THE DANGEROUS
INHERITANCE

THE DANGEROUS INHERITANCE

IZOLA FORRESTER

or, The Mystery of the Tittani Rubies

wildsidepress.com

WILDSIDE PRESS

Originally published 1919-1920.
Published by Wildside Press LLC.
wildsidepress.com

CHAPTER I

The town studio of Signor Jacobelli faced the west. It was situated on the top floor of an old eight-storied building in the West Fifties. Thirty years ago this had been given over entirely to studios, but now it was broken up into a more profitable mêlée of semi-commercial establishments and light-housekeeping apartments.

The signor, having no doubt the Old-World propensity for permanency, had maintained his studio here for over twenty years, without regard for the changing conditions around him, if indeed he were even conscious of them. His own immediate outlook and environment had remained the same. The view to the west and south from the deep, double-sized windows had varied little, and held a perpetual fascination for him. Thin red chimneys in neighborly groupings on adjacent roofs assumed delicate color values of amethyst and quivering saffrons from Jersey sunsets that turned even the old buildings down towards the riverfront into mystical genii palaces in the early twilight.

Dust lay unnoted upon bookshelves and music-racks about the large, friendly room. The Turkish rug that covered its floor had long since lost all outline of pattern and was as exquisite a blur as the rose-flushed sea mist that hung over the lower end of the island city.

Carlota stood in a window recess, her back to the signor and his unexpected guest, her fingers tying and untying the faded purple silk cord of the shade. From where he sat in the old winged armchair by the piano, Ward caught a perfect silhouette of her profile against the glow of western light. Listening to Jacobelli's fiery protest in his usual silent way, his mind dwelt upon the blossoming of this foreign flower of girlhood who had so strangely attracted him from the first time he had ever looked into her eyes.

The Marchese Veracci had called him up from the Italian Club two years before, and had besought his good offices for the granddaughter of Margherita Paoli. The following evening they had called on him by appointment. He half closed his eyes, recalling the picture of the girl as he had first seen her. They awaited him in the Florentine room. Even then she had not thought of him, but had stood before a painting of Sorrento, a view through the ravine looking seaward, one hand laid on her breast, her eyes filled with the yearning of youth's loneliness. She had met him silently, her hand cold as it rested an instant in his palm.

And the old Marchese had pleaded her cause with fervent eloquence.

"I have Jacobelli's word on her voice," he said. "What more would you? If you but speak Guido Jacobelli's name to any European director, he bows to the old maestro's dictum."

"He has retired," Ward returned.

"Retired, yes, from the money mart." The Marchese had beamed upon the great international banker almost tolerantly. "You cannot comprehend his attitude. No amount of money could tempt him to teach the tyro, the climber, but he has heard Carlota. He knew Paoli well in Italy. It was her influence and friendship which first brought him fame and power. Now he has said that her voice lives again in the child, but there must be at least four years of incessant application and training. To keep her voice divine, she must never be troubled by material cares. She must have an abundance of everything that she needs that her whole nature may relax and expand to give her the freedom to devote her whole life to her career."

Ward had understood. He knew Guido Jacobelli. While the old maestro was a high priest of art, his price for teaching genius was in proportion to his faith. It had been Carlota's own attitude of indifference which had dominated his decision. While the Marchese had argued and pleaded for her future, and Maria Roma, her guardian, had hung upon the final word from Ward's lips, she had listened gravely, her attention wandering constantly to the rare art treasures of the room. Once she had met his eyes as he asked her a direct question.

"You are very young to study seriously. Do you realize the sacrifices you must make?"

"I have always studied to be a singer, signor," Carlota had told him, her eyes even then disconcerting in their wide intensity. "There are no sacrifices when you love your vocation."

Ward had smiled back at the Marchese, quoting lightly:

"I did renounce the world, its pride and greed
...at eight years old."

"My dear," he added, "one of your own countrymen has spoken so, Fra Lippo Lippi. No parallel, though, eh, Veracci? Here we have the consecration of genius. I will advance fifty thousand. Is it enough?"

Carlota had met his appraising eyes with the aloof resentment of an influence that disturbed her.

"Speak, cara mia," Maria Roma had cried, tears streaming down her plump cheeks, as she clasped her arms enthusiastically around her charge. "Have you no word of thanks?"

And Ward had never forgotten the flash of challenge in the girl's dark eyes as she had given him her hand.

"I will succeed and pay you back, signor," she had said. He might have been merely a money-lender to a princess of the de' Medici.

He had made only one stipulation and that half in jest, though Maria and the Marchese had agreed most earnestly. She was not to marry nor become entangled in love affairs during the period of her tuition. The concession had completely escaped Carlota's attention. She had wandered by them out into the wide corridor, stifled by the somber silence of the great closed rooms. Not a single fountain falling in the distance, not a living flower anywhere, nothing but age-old treasures in a palatial, modern museum. He had not spoken to her again, only she had heard his last words to Jacobelli.

"May the fruit fulfill the promise. I will come to see you now and then."

Through the two years of study he had kept his word. Every few months, unawares, he would come to the old studio and sit for a while, listening to Jacobelli and watching his pupil. Even while he never spoke a word of direct intent to her, Carlota felt a vague uneasiness in his presence, under the steady power of his gaze. He carried with him the impression of a compelling, dominant masterfulness, all the more irresistible through its silence and tireless patience. He was in the late thirties at this time, tall and heavy-set, his head, with its thick, close-cut blond hair, thrust forward from a habit of silent intentness. There was the strongest suggestion of the leonine about him. Once, when she was a child, Carlota remembered being taken to see a captive Algerian lion that had just been brought across for the royal zoo. With a city mob surging forward to stare at him, the lion had lain with an imperial languor and indifference, gazing with unblinking eyes beyond the crowd and the city, seeing only the desert that held his whole life's desire. Sometimes, in the studio, during one of Ward's visits, she would catch his eyes fixed upon her, while Jacobelli flamed out into some argument or dissertation, and she would shrink from the purpose that lay behind their patience.

Today the voice of Jacobelli filled the studio, and Carlota's delicate dark brows contracted sharply as she listened.

"What more can I do? I have given her all that I know of technique and harmony, and still her voice lacks that emotional quality which the greatest alone possess. The divine voice must have dramatic feeling, intensity. It must lose itself in the grandest passion of emotion. The child tries, but what would you? She does not understand the lack in her own nature. Her woman soul yet slumbers."

Ward glanced at him with amused, quizzical eyes.

"Let it sleep, Jacobelli. Remember Paoli when she let love conquer her."

For the moment the old maestro forgot the figure behind the window curtain. With arms thrown upward he turned on the banker.

"You know not anything about Paoli! I, Jacobelli, tell you that! You cannot speak of her with any understanding. She was a law to herself in her own generation. Few women can be that. But I, who know what lay behind the wall of Tittani, say to you I would rather this child lay dead now, with no fulfillment in her life, than that she should know the agony and failure as an artiste that her grandmother did when she sacrificed her whole womanhood—for what? Love, pouf!"

"Can a woman's nature reach its ripest fulfillment without love?" Ward's tone was lowered. "History proves that the greatest geniuses have been those who suffered most."

"But not the singer, signor." Jacobelli paused in his march up and down the studio. "The singer is something different. It is instinctive. I have heard the most marvelous impassioned voices pour from the most commonplace peasant types. I have heard the greatest tenor of all times tear the emotions of thousands to pieces, and step into his dressing-room to rail at his wife for not providing his favorite dish for him after the opera, ravioli and lampreys. The most superb lyric voice of today comes from a little, stout contadina who picked up centimes around the flower-market in Naples when I was young. Do you think she acquired divinity of soul and utterance from some supreme emotion? Ridiculous. She is a gourmand, a virago, absolutely bourgeois, yet she sings like a seraph. Why, then, is it not in Carlota's voice?"

Ward rose leisurely. The old silken curtains hung motionless. The shadows were heavy in the corners of the studio.

"She is a higher type," he said in a low voice. "When you agree with me, bring her to me."

CHAPTER II

After Ward had gone the old Italian maestro seated himself at the piano, improvising as he always did when he was disturbed. It was an enormous old ebony instrument, mellow and vibrant in its response to his touch. He did not even look up as Carlota leaned her elbows upon a pile of dusty folios, watching him anxiously. Finally she drew a quick, impatient breath.

"I wish he would never come here again."

"It is customary," Jacobelli shrugged his expansive shoulders. "You are too sensitive, my dear. It is you who are conferring a favor in permitting this person to provide the means for your education. You will return to him, in the hour of your triumph, every penny it has been his privilege to advance at this time."

"Why does he come here and sit looking at me in such a way? In the courtyard at home there were little lizards that came out early in the morning, gray and cold, with eyes like his, green in the light. I was always afraid of putting my hand on one of them around the fountain."

Jacobelli struck a minor chord, avoiding her eyes.

"Because he is a man, and you are growing beautiful. You will become accustomed to this sort of thing. All men will love you, or seem to. It is the compliment paid to women who are great artistes. Your grandmother was adored in her day. Kings and princes knelt at her shrine, and fought for her favor. Even I was infatuated with her. You must learn to smile impersonally and receive homage."

"Then it is not—love?" Carlota asked doubtfully. "I heard what you said to him about her. Why did you say that, about her suffering and sacrifice? I never remember her like that. She was wonderful. She seemed to give out radiance and warmth like the sunlight. Wasn't she happy?"

Jacobelli's hands were flung up suddenly, and he laughed at her.

"My dear, who may say when a woman is happy or when she is not. Sometimes they find their greatest happiness in their most supreme suffering. She was divine, that is enough. As for love, Carlotina mia, it is merely Life's plaything. It is the toy we give to youth, but never, never to genius. The rabble amuses itself with what it calls love. But genius is sufficient unto itself. It is the celestial fire. It does not seek a mortal torch upon its altar."

"You said you would rather see me dead—" began Carlota slowly, when the little electric bell at the outer door rang lightly, announcing Maria Roma at her customary hour of five. As always, she followed it by half opening the door, peering around with an arch, reconnoitering glance.

"Do I intrude?" she asked, with her beaming smile, and entered impressively, always with the dramatic action as if the orchestra had sounded her motif. She shook one forefinger impressively at Carlota. "You loiter and take up the maestro's time, gossip and loiter when you should be studying."

But Jacobelli waved aside the admonition with one ample movement of his large, plump hand. As Carlota went to the inner room for her cloak and hat, he spoke in an undertone.

"Ward is becoming very much interested in her. She treats him with indifference. You must teach her diplomacy. She has too much arrogance of youth, and absolutely no gratitude for what he is doing for her."

Maria's brilliant dark eyes narrowed with comprehensive amusement.

"You ask the impossible, Guido. I who have known all three, Margherita, Bianca, and this glorious child, tell you the truth, and you will remember what I say. You can no more teach the heart of a Paoli to keep its temperament within bounds than you can yoke the thunder-clouds and lightning that sweep down over our Trentino."

"And the responsibility is ours," said Jacobelli, with a deep exhalation of his cigarette. "Given this nature, we are to keep her a prisoner behind the wall of Tittani, eh?"

Maria sank deeply into the velvet-cushioned chair beside him, and the two smiled at each other reminiscently.

"It was a high wall," she sighed at length. "I remember your last visit there, Guido, before the child was born, five years I think it was. Bianca was a flower then. Such flaming hair and dark eyes, the true Florentine type. She was more like Tittani in her looks. Carlota is a throwback to the grandmother. Ah, my Guido, was there ever a woman like her? Even at the last, before he died, when her heart was torn with agony of renunciation—"

"She lost her voice," Jacobelli spoke with finality. "Yet Ward would tell me love is the great fulfillment. Did she ever sing again? No. She buried her art with her love in the grave of her poet after he had denied her to the world. You and I, Maria Roma, who know of this, must protect this child against the traitor in her own nature."

Maria sighed doubtfully. She was the large, vivid type of the Italian peasant, richly developed by success and circumstance. Years before, Sforza, director of La Scala, had journeyed with friends to a mountain section of the Trentino. In the purple twilight a voice had drifted down to them from a band of vintage workers, homeward bound. It was Maria Roma at eighteen, a buoyant, deep-breasted bacchante, her black hair hanging in thick clusters of curls around her radiant face.

Enrico Sforza had loved her, more perhaps for her ardent faithfulness and responsiveness. She had achieved a sensation in contralto rôles and he had interested La Paoli in his peasant love. In middle age, after his death, Maria had retired to live at the Villa Tittani with the old diva. Here she had shared with her in the tragedy of her final years. Fifty years before, the story of Margherita Paoli and her love for John Tennant, the English poet, had been part of the romance of Italy. Her beauty and genius had opened every door of success to her. Even on the threshold of womanhood she had been given all that ambition could demand from life, and turning in the highest hour of her triumphs, she had forsaken the world for a year, giving the full gift of her love to Tennant.

Suddenly she had returned, restless and hungering for her art. As Maria knew, Tennant had been jealous of her voice and the life which he could not share, had demanded that she give up her career for the sake of their love, and return with him to England. And she had laughed at him. Love could not bring full completeness and happiness to a woman of genius, she had said. It could not satisfy her for the loss of the divine fire. Tennant had left Italy, and five years later she married Count Tittani. Bianca, the mother of Carlota, had been born at the old villa overlooking the Campagna. She had spent her childhood here, and in the convent of Maria Pietà at the head of the ancient ilex avenue leading up from Mondragone. Tittani had died when she was nine, leaving La Paoli the prestige of his name and wealth combined with her own full measure of maturity in her art.

It was at this time that Maria had come nearest to her confidence. Word came from England to them that Tennant had been stricken blind, and in the midst of a gala performance of "Traviata," La Paoli had left all and gone to him. He had refused to see her when she reached London. Bertrand Wallace, his closest friend, had told her simply enough that he was without means, that he longed to go to Italy where "he might feel the sun on his face," and she had entered into the splendid conspiracy that glorified the end of her life.

The Villa Tittani faced the Campagna with a lofty, blank wall. Beyond it stretched terraced gardens, winding alleys of cypress and ilexes, a place of enchantment, with the never-ending music of falling waters in the distance, of hidden fountains in grottoes, and cascades that fell over ancient steps in ripples of silver. Yet all its beauty was dominated by its wall, blank on one side, terraced on the garden side into long, steep depths of mystery, of infinite green vistas that lost their way in the cypress gloom of the lower distances.

Here Wallace brought his friend, the blind poet, to the little house near the end of the wall where the view opened seaward. Two old servants of the Tittani had cared for him until his passing, and here La Paoli could come and watch him from a distance, unseen or suspected in the largesse of her love by the man whose faith she had betrayed for fame. It was characteristic of her that even in her grief and isolation from him, she seemed to find a supreme, almost fierce, satisfaction in the tragic immolation of her own happiness for his sake. He had died finally, unconscious, on her breast, and she had never sung again.

"You see, Maria, I have proved the truth of it in my own heart's blood," she had said, "A woman cannot serve two gods. If Bianca has my voice, help me to teach her this: no man is content with half of a woman's love or nature. If she desires to attain to the highest art, she must sacrifice love."

Within six months after she had left the shelter of the convent Bianca had married Peppino Trelango, son of a dead patriot. The Contessa had cared for him through his boyhood, because she had heard him playing on his violin once on the old quay at Pontecova where centuries before the body of the boy count, Giovanni Borgia, had borne witness against his brother in the dawn. When Bianca came home, she had met him in the old gardens, a boy of nineteen, like one of the marble fauns come to life to teach her youth's heritage. When the Contessa returned from a trip to her favorite midsummer retreat at Isola Bella, she had found the two gone, and Maria desolate with despair.

It was from this romance that Carlota had been born. After the death of Peppino in an Algerian skirmish, Bianca had returned to the villa behind the old rose-colored wall with her child. She had lived in the gardens with the memories of her love, a silent, smiling, stately girl who baffled the vivid, emotional La Paoli by the elusive sensitiveness of her nature.

"She is the wraith of my passion for the love I denied," the Contessa would declare. "I starved for him, and trampled the desire with my pride while I bore her to Tittani. She is the very spirit of renunciation, Maria, and she will drive me to madness with her silence and resignation. Carlota is not like her. She is a flame, a beautiful rosebud, all light and movement. She is like I was, God keep her."

Carlota was four when they bore her mother down to the old tomb of the Tittani. She could remember her voice at night when she bent over her to kiss her, and the fall of her long, soft hair over her face. Sometimes in their walks through the gardens, in the quiet years of her girlhood, she would come to the old tomb set into the hillside, its iron gates overgrown with vines, and she would lean her cheek against them. Assunta, her nurse, would scold her for not keeping her thoughts on the spiritual.

"Ah, a little that was my mother lies here," Carlota would answer. "I may love it, Assunta, without sinning, may I not, just her beautiful hair even?"

After Italy entered the war, the villa had been turned into a hospital, and the fortune of the Contessa laid at the feet of "La Patria."

"Still, there is some left," she had told Maria at the time of her own departure. Strong in spirit and dominant, she had ruled to the end, planning and directing Carlota's future. "I have given the child a heritage and training that are priceless. If you have to, sell the jewels in the cinque cento chest. They are for her. I have not even looked at them since he died. Take her to America, Maria. Find there Guido Jacobelli. He was a boy when I made my début, before your time, the gala performance of *Rigoletto*. I was a wonderful Gilda, Maria. Later I gave him his first start. He is not one who forgets. You will go to him in New York and he will find you a patron. I have written to the Marchese Veracci to expect you and see that you are lodged fittingly. No economy. Surround her with beauty and comfort while she studies, but keep her from love until she has won success. Her mother sacrificed all for Peppino's kiss. If I were able I would keep her here behind the wall of Tittani and never let her see the face of a man whom she might love. Dust and ashes all, Maria. The greatest and most enduring is the memory of a lost love."

After the closing of the old villa, Carlota and Signora Roma had come to New York. Maria had been prodigal in her expenditures. She had taken an expensive studio and had lavished the tenderest care on her charge.

"The art quarters of Europe, cara mia," she would say to her airily when Carlota protested, "have been filled for generations with what?—failures. Boy and girl aspirants, pitiful little garret Pierrots and Columbines, starving upon hopes that never materialized. Art is greedy. It demands all of your nerve, force and vitality. To come out of the training of the next four years a victor, you must pamper yourself. Dress well, eat well, feed your love of beauty as well as your stomach. Remember, 'white hyacinths for the soul as well as bread for the body.' You will be a slave to your art, and must keep the fires burning."

"But you will use up all we have," Carlota had protested.

"What then?" Maria had demanded proudly. "You have only a small fortune left. You must have thousands, tens of thousands before you bow to your first night's audience."

They had met the old Marchese Veracci the first week of their arrival. Few there were in the Washington Square section of the city who were not familiar with the stately Old-World figure of the Marchese. He was as welcome in the crowded Sicilian quarter below Fourth Street as in the corridors of the Brevoort or Lafayette. He held his court daily at the fountain in the center of the Square. Always with a fresh boutonnière and a smile and courtly word for every dark-eyed child who laughed back at him. Sometimes, when he strolled past the bust of Garibaldi, he would leave a little spray of flowers on the pedestal. After dinner he never failed to stroll out into the twilight and lift his soul in salute to the cross of light that gleamed on the memorial tower above the trees.

"It is the one spot in the whole city," he told them, "that holds the Old-World glamour and charm, yet I would not have you and Carlota living down here. The lines of demarcation are too blurred between the workers and the dreamers. Then, too, there are the dancing shapes that come to stare and ridicule. There is a contagion of play here that breaks the concentration you must put into your study, my child. Keep away from it at this period. Later, I could wish you nothing better than to share in the spirit of comradeship in art and beauty, yes, and most of all, in humanity. That you will find down here, no matter how others try to detract from the atmosphere, like the very small boys who will ever toss pebbles at the stained-glass windows of the saints."

Maria Roma had agreed fervently to anything he said. His delighted enthusiasm satisfied her that the old Contessa had chosen rightly in making him joint guardian with her over Carlota. Guido Jacobelli had retired, he had told her over their first luncheon en tête-à-tête at the Italian Club. Money would never tempt him to teach. Nothing but brilliant genius in a pupil could ever lure him from his retreat to give them the full benefit of his years of experience and study.

"I know him well, and of them all he is still the wizard, the maestro. Even now, his word on a voice would open the gates of opportunity to any singer. Casanova, of the Opera here, bows to his dictum. If it were anybody but Margherita Paoli who calls to me, I would say no, but as it is, ma bella, we will go. Two places I know where we may find him, at his old studio in town and his country home at Arrochar, on Staten Island. We will go there."

The visit had proven Carlota's crucial hour. Maria had hovered over her excitedly, feeling that upon the great old maestro's verdict lay the entire future fate of her career. The Marchese had called for them and had accompanied them out to Jacobelli's home. It was typical of his simplicity and love of nature. On the wooded heights above Kill von Kull at Arrochar, lay a small colony of Italian artists and musicians. Their homes were like miniature villas perched above a smaller bay of Naples when the myriad lights gleamed on the shipping and distant Jersey hills.

As they walked up the quiet hill street from the station, Carlota's dark eyes had sparkled with memories. Surely in this perfect fall day, with the vivid blue of a cloudless sky above the deep crimson and gold of autumn foliage, there was a semblance of the Villa Tittani's beauty. A rock wall covered with brilliant red creeper vines surrounded the garden. It seemed neglected, with shrubbery straggling in groups, unclipped and straying. The stone flower urns were overgrown with rank, clambering vines. In the southeast corner a dancing faun poised with wary, pointed ears, as if listening seaward. When the Marchese tried to open the outer vestibule door of the enclosed veranda, two stately Italian greyhounds rose leisurely and eyed the callers questioningly.

Within they had found Jacobelli living alone with his memories. Carlota never forgot the picture that he made, welcoming them into his wide, sunlit studio. Swarthy, stout, curly-haired, frowning at her from heavy eyebrows, he had seemed to gauge and grasp her whole capabilities in one swift, cursory glance. She had been caressed and encouraged all of her life, but now, for the first time, she felt her confidence shaken as she waited by the piano, facing the piercing eyes and uncompromising glare of the old maestro. Never once, during the two years of study under him that followed that first visit, had she shaken off that first impression. Eccentric, proud, profoundly conscious of his power to make or unmake queens of the operatic world, he had been a revelation to her from that day.

The Marchese had pleaded for her eloquently, showing the letter he had received from La Paoli a few weeks before her death. Jacobelli had listened to it in silence, staring fixedly at the girl. She was very like her grandmother in appearance, he thought. Behind her stood a towering old terra-cotta jar filled with scarlet autumn leaves. She looked out at the sea view, her eyes filled with a dreaming longing. Her hair was heavy and lustrous, growing back from a low, broad forehead with the shell-like outline one sees in the portraits of Beatrice or one of Del Sarto's girl saints. Her eyes were long and shadowy, heavy-lidded, aloof. When she was interested or startled, they opened widely, a deep, warm brown color, their darkness made more vivid by the rare rose red of her lips and the peculiar jasmine clearness of her skin. But it was something beyond mere beauty and grace that arrested Jacobelli's interest. There was a sense of suppressed vitality about her, the insistent promise of the unusual, of some compelling magnetism that lay behind her silence and repression. Suddenly he seated himself at the long bench, and struck a chord for her pitch.

"Sing," he ordered. "First, a long scale."

Carlota had hesitated, looking to Maria for sympathy. Might she not sing, for this supreme trial, some famous aria? But Signora Roma had raised both hands in hushed rebuke. They were before the final tribunal. The outcome was on the knees of the gods. But as the full, vibrant soprano rose to the scale, Jacobelli struck a crashing chord and leapt from the bench, clasping his arms about the slim figure at his side.

"Ah, Sanctissima Maria, it is there!" he shouted. "It is the voice of Paoli come to life once more! My beautiful, my marvel, ah, what we will not make of you! Sing, cara mia, sing again for me. No, so!"

For over an hour Carlota sang for him, while Maria sat by the deep bay window, weeping from sheer happiness, and the old Marchese strolled to and fro, stroking the greyhounds, and smoking incessantly, keeping time as he smiled at the success of his experiment.

The fruition of that first visit had come richly in the two years that followed it. Carlota was eighteen now, with not alone the years of her grandmother's careful teaching, but Jacobelli's unceasing discipline and watchfulness as her voice ripened and developed. One year more and she would be ready for her début, he said. It was this final year she dreaded, with Ward's visits to the studio becoming more frequent and his interest in her losing its cloak of patronage.

She was silent on this day, almost during the entire homeward walk across the Park. Their apartment had been Maria's choice, selected against the better judgment of even the Marchese. He had advised a smaller, less expensive suite farther uptown, but in a conservative section. Maria had cast the suggestion from her scornfully. For the struggling student any environment was of secondary consideration, but for the sole pupil of Guido Jacobelli, the protégée of Ogden Ward, there must be a gilded cage. Between Fifth Avenue and Madison in the upper Sixties she had found one that suited her, a spacious apartment that in its richness of tone satisfied her. It might have been from the Villa Tittani itself, by the time Maria had finished its decoration.

"You had worried the maestro today," she said severely, as they approached the heavy bronze and crystal entrance. "He could not even improvise. We are giving our whole hearts and souls to you for your success, and you are not grateful."

Carlota turned her head and smiled at her tenderly. She was used to the scoldings of the old prima donna.

"I am grateful to you, tanta mia," she said, slipping her hand under the other's arm. "But I sometimes think I hate Mr. Ward. When I hear his footstep I cannot sing any more, and when he sits there and looks at me I could jump from the window. I hate his eyes and his voice and everything about him."

Maria's dark eyebrows arched in amazement. She glanced with quick suspicion at the girl's troubled face.

"But you have no reason—have you?"

Carlota's eyes narrowed with amusement at her anxiety. As they entered the lower hall, she stripped off her long gray suède gloves impatiently. The lights were not switched on yet, and she let one fall near the outer steps. It lay, a part of the twilight, unnoticed by either herself or Maria, but one who came behind them picked it up. It was a mere fleeting impression she caught of him. Maria had stepped into the elevator when he reached her side to return it, a curious, poster-like figure, with the uncertain light accentuating his foreign features and half-closed, seeking eyes.

"Yes, it is mine, thank you," she said gravely, and carried with her upstairs an impression of restless, suppressed dissent and discontent combined with a haunting fragrance of a new cigarette smoke. When she reached the apartment, while Maria hurried to make Russian tea for them, she stood by the window, looking down over the boxes of green. Across the street in the mother-of-pearl gloom, she could see the glow of the cigarette where the boy stood, waiting for something, and it held her with almost a premonition of menace.

CHAPTER III

Over the tea she was unusually silent, while Maria, ensconced at last on her favorite chaise longue, mellowed under the warmth. Carlota's voice, cool with daring, broke in on her relaxation.

"Maria, when will you treat me as a woman?"

Maria's face flushed as she spilled the tea blindly on the rug.

"You are in love?" she gasped. "Never would you have thought of such a thing if you were not in love."

"Oh, you poor, old preciosa!" Carlota laughed richly, folding her arms around the signora's ample shoulders. "I wouldn't know love if I met him face to face this minute in your teacup. But I want to know so much, Maria. I want to ask you about so many things. You love me, do you not? Enough to tell me anything at all I ask you?"

"Ah, do I not," sighed Maria uneasily. "Is it about Mr. Ward?"

Carlota drew up a low footstool of rose silk and ivory carving, and laid her glossy head close to the one on the pillows.

"I have said I hate him," she replied composedly. "Let us forget that I ever have to see him again. I want you to listen and love me more than you ever have so you will answer me truthfully. Why did Signor Jacobelli tell Mr. Ward today that my grandmother sacrificed her whole womanhood and that he would rather see me dead than have me like her. What was behind the wall of Tittani that I never knew about?"

"He is a pompous old egoist," Maria answered with amazing composure considering the tumult in her mind. "You remember her? Did she not live like a queen with her court even at her age? She was the most regal person I ever knew. You can remember the life at the villa? Was it somber or full of unhappiness? She was the Contessa Tittani. She had everything she wanted. Some day when you have gained all that she did, we will go back to the old villa, and spend our summers there. Remember your goats, beloved, the little Nini and Cherubini—"

"They will be gone when we get back," Carlota said slowly. "You have lied to me as you always do, Maria, with love. I will tell you things I remember that you do not know I know. I can remember my mother. She was very white, with eyes like the lower pool in the moonlight, and her hair was so soft and so long. I felt it always over my face in the darkness when she bent to kiss me good-night. I have dreamt I felt it since, and wakened reaching for her. You know Assunta?"

Maria murmured an inarticulate, doubtful injunction to Assunta's attendant dæmon, and made horns with her finger-tips with a subconscious reversion to the old superstition of the Trentino fireside tales.

"She had a rattling tongue. What has she told you?"

"It was about the wall." Carlota clasped her hands around her knees, and looked before her seeing the way of the old villa and the beauty of it. "It was so high to me in those days. I have looked up at it, Maria, until it seemed as if its highest terrace met the sky."

"There were seven, built by Giovanni Fontana."

"I loved them. The stone was so old and rose-colored with green and violet streaking it. On the side towards the road it was so bare and forbidding, and on our side it was all beauty and lavishness as if it could not give us too much, of its bounty. There was no entrance, you remember, Maria, there by the road, and I used to follow the wall around the garden trying to see how you ever went out through it. And Assunta told me, I suppose to keep me satisfied, that no one had ever found the way over the wall excepting my mother—"

"Ah, the blind, cackling pullet. If I had known—" Maria nodded her head with relish. "She was selling melons in Mondragone when your mother lived."

"And when I asked her how my mother ever climbed the wall"—Carlota's eyes closed and opened again with dreamy ecstasy—"she told me she escaped with the wings of love. After that—don't scold, dear, I love to talk to you about it, and there is no one else now—after that I loved the wall better than all the gardens and the fountains and the grottoes even. Won't you tell me what Jacobelli meant, now? What meaning did he put into it all, the wall and the unhappiness of my grandmother and the tragedy of it all?"

Maria Roma was silent for some time. Slowly she reached for a cigarette and lighted it, drawing deeply on it as she stared upward at the ceiling.

"I have waited for this," she said finally, with a sigh of resignation. "Some day I knew you would ask me, and out of all the world, I would rather tell you, because I will discriminate between what you should know and what is best buried in that old garden tomb. Wait." She pushed away Carlota's reaching arms. "See what I have saved for you out of the past."

Impulsively she rose and crossed to the end of the studio. Hidden here behind old strips of tapestry and mediæval embroidery were old locked chests which had been brought from Italy with all the care the dower treasures of a princess might have commanded. Carlota had never even guessed at their contents. If she had given the matter a thought at all, she had believed them filled with little household keepsakes, linen, silver, bric-à-brac which Maria had managed to save for her.

Now she stood in amazement as the old singer lifted out costume after costume from the chests, stage raiment and festive gowns of thirty and forty years before. From carved and inlaid boxes she drew out gems and decorations that had been lavished on the great diva and laid them before Carlota, forgetting in the pride of the moment the discretion of silence regarding the romance of genius. The girl's eyes widened with glowing wonder and delight as she fingered the old treasures, listening to Maria's vivid, picturesque recital of the reign of Margherita Paoli.

"She was taller than you, cara mia, majestic, a queen in carriage and expression. She never wore other hair than her own. It was golden bronze and hung in ripples to her knees. I have woven it in Marguerita's plaits with these strands of pearls, and coiled it high into Fedora's crown with this diamond and ruby tiara. The necklace is here, too." She piled the contents of the cases eagerly until she found it. "Rubies and diamonds. They came from the crown jewels of Roumania, a part of the Constantinople loot centuries ago. The crown prince was exiled to a mountain garrison in the Caucasus for two years after he gave them to her, but he never told where they were. This center ruby in the tiara is from Persia, one of the finest in the world. Some day you shall wear them. They will suit you as they did her. And this—ah, my child, you should have seen her wearing this in *Semiramide*." She lifted out a heavy barbaric stomacher encrusted in rough, uncut jewels. "This was given to her by the Rajah of Kadurstan. He tried to kill himself after the performance one night in Paris when she refused to see him. This necklace of opals and emeralds was from the Grand Duke of Teklahava. It had been part of the Byzantine loot in the days of Ivan the Terrible. Ah, but, Carlota, behold, this was ever about her throat, the medallion hidden in her breast from all eyes. Never will I forget the night when Tennant gave it to her. The king had given a farewell banquet for her. She was decorated and fêted as never any other singer was. And after it was over, I saw the two as they stood out in the moonlit loggia of the palace, and he clasped this about her white throat. His portrait is in the medallion. There is a secret spring—wait—so it opens. Was he not a worthy lover for her?"

Carlota looked long at the pictured face in the old gold and crystal case. It was old-fashioned in style. The hair was worn long and curled back thickly from his forehead. It was the head of an enthusiast, boyish, too, in its eager intensity, passionate, unsatisfied.

"He does not look happy," she said slowly. "I have never heard his name before. Who was he, Maria?"

Signora slipped from the clouds with a shock of reality and caught the medallion from her hand.

"No one, no one at all. See this ring, one single perfect solitaire surrounded by black pearls, a gift from the Empress of France, my child."

Carlota rose, staring down at the wealth of jewels with puzzled, hurt pride.

"Why have we accepted money from Mr. Ward to pay for my tuition when we had these to sell?"

The vandalism of the suggestion horrified Maria. She replaced everything with a resolute hand, locking each case from a small bunch of keys suspended from a slender chain on her neck.

"You would market the trophies of your grandmother!" she said haughtily. "America has commercialized you. They belong to the woman you will be. I will give you the keys at your début."

"I don't care so very much for them. They are beautiful, but, after all, they are only things you buy. I asked you for something richer."

She laid her arms coaxingly about Maria's throat. "Was my mother happy?"

"If love can make any woman happy, she was." Signora Roma's voice broke with agitation. "Do not ask me anything further."

"She was very young to die, was she not, only twenty-two? She was younger than I am now when she first met my father, wasn't she, Maria?" No answer, but she felt the tears on her own cheek as she pressed it to Maria's face. "I think I know what it is you will not tell me. With all the jewels and triumphs, my grandmother lost her love, and somehow, my mother found love even though she died so young and was never famous. Is that it?"

Maria suddenly reached her hands upward and framed the face above her in a tremulous caress.

"You have the heritage of rebellion; how can I warn you or teach you to fight it? Your worst enemy, Carlota, is your own heart. Distrust it. It is the traitor to your individuality—your genius, whatever you like to call it."

Carlota stood erect, laughing suddenly, her arms outstretched widely.

"Listen to this that Assunta told me too," she said teasingly. "Once, hundreds of years ago, the Villa Tittani was part of an old castle. The wall is all that is left of it, and the old tower above the grottoes. And there was a Princess Fiametta—"

Maria made horns with her finger-tips hastily.

"Assunta was a scandalous waggle-tongue. Had I only guessed that she was stuffing your ears with this sort of gunpowder, I would have known how to finish her forever. I hear the bell."

It was the Marchese, courtly and whimsical as he glanced shrewdly from one to the other.

"I have come to entreat a favor," he said happily. "After I have partaken of your most excellent tea, ma bella Maria, I will ask it. I have not the courage yet. How is our little one?"

Carlota's brows drew together behind his back. She waited in silence, listening while the Marchese brought Maria into a mellow mood with his little buoyant stories and high lights of adventure.

"Ah, but I have seen sights today, a whole avenue of traffic held up because a tiny goldfinch escaped from a bird store on Twenty-Third Street. It alighted directly in the car track and shrank there panting and terrified, and in this hard-hearted, prosaic city, not one would drive over it. Is not that a fair sign of the times, my friend? And again, I take the 'bus down the Avenue at dusk for the beauty of the lights in perspective, like magnolia blooms if you but half close your eyes. And yesterday I saw the conductor, a red-cheeked Irish boy, reading a newspaper that had been left on a seat. What you think? The baseball column? The sports? Not at all." The Marchese chuckled tenderly. "He reads the advice to young mothers. See? It is the brand new bambino somewhere with its finger-tips rose-petaled, holding his heart fast. And a pack of children on Thompson Street fighting—for what? A trampled pink carnation. I would have turned them loose if I could have, in that meadow of oleanders and the orange grove beyond, you remember, Maria, as you come down from Frascati and below the Campagna and the sea. Salute!" He sighed reminiscently, and reached for his teacup. "I am an old romanticist, Carlota. Your youth must be patient with my maunderings of sentiment."

Maria retired to the kitchenette to prepare fresh tea, and Carlota lighted the candles on the low table by the fire.

"You are happy, yes?" the Marchese asked, regarding her with the pride he took no pains to conceal. "Jacobelli tells me it may only be for one year more, and then, behold! I live for that first night of triumph."

Carlota sighed impatiently. It was as though the sight of the jewels and story of La Paoli's life had wakened in her youth's urge for adventure. She looked up at the fine old face wistfully.

"I am lonely. Tanta keeps me as secluded as if I were in a convent. Surely I am old enough to go out somewhere. Now that summer is over, it seems as if I could not stand another winter. Aren't they bleak here? Every day when we walk in the Park, I want to turn and run from it all, the stripped trees and caged animals, and Maria and Jacobelli, and everything!" Her finger-tips stretched widely. "I am homesick."

"No, you are just ennuied, that is all," said the Marchese soothingly. He pursed his lips until his silver-gray imperial and pointed mustache took on the semblance of a crescent and scimitar. Yet his eyes twinkled down at her understandingly. "Sunday evening I go, as is my custom, to the home of my friend Carrollton Phelps. Many,

many interesting people drop in there at that time. It would be a beginning for you, but, mind, I will not have you known for what you
are. Not a whisper."

"Are they all"—Carlota checked herself; not for worlds would
she have wounded the debonnair old courtier by even suggesting that
he was past the meridian of life—"famous?"

"No, no, no. They are all aspirants," he corrected. "One must
show some signs of having the germ, at least, of genius before the
door opens widely, but you will find many who are young like yourself, many. I, myself, will prepare Maria."

But when the evening came the signora was indisposed, and insisted on Carlota's remaining with her. The Marchese waved her ob-
jections aside tenderly.

"It is most informal and Mrs. Phelps is charming. Here in America, Maria, we adjust the barriers of etiquette to the whim of the moment. I will guard her from anything dangerous, you may be sure."

They had taken a hansom down the avenue, instead of a taxi. It
was the Marchese's choice.

"I never like to be hurried," he told her. "I do not like this—what
do they call it?—joy of speeding. The aeroplane, yes. I have two
boys in the service at home, but not for amusement. I like to take my
little moments of outdoor enjoyment leisurely. You will see, my dear,
how beautiful this is. I call it my avenue of flower lights."

The home of the Phelpses was on East Tenth Street, a tall four-
storied residence of dark brown stone. Above the low deep French
doorway there stretched across the entire second floor a great carved
Moorish window of exquisite fretwork which Phelps had transported
from an old palace in Seville.

Despite her indisposition Maria had given much thought and
anxiety to Carlota's toilette for the occasion. Finally, she had laid out
for her a beautiful old scarf of Point Venise, so yellowed by age that
it was the tint of old ivory. It was encrusted with tiny seed pearls,
and with it she selected from one of the chests a girdle of gold links,
cunningly joined in serpentine fashion with pendent topaz here and
there.

"It is a trifle too barbaric," she had mused, "but yet it suits you.
And you shall wear white velvet like Julietta."

"Oh, no, I will not," laughed Carlota, kissing her. "You would have me perpetually making my début, tanta." Accordingly she had chosen her own gown, the hue of an oak autumn leaf, which fell close to her slender young figure in mediæval lines. As she lingered before the mirror before leaving, Carlota smiled back at her reflection almost with a challenge. Back at the villa there was an old painting hanging at a turn in a staircase, where the sunlight would fall full upon it from an oriel window high above. It was the Princess Fiametta, her eyes wearied with the weight of the golden crown that bound her brows, her gown the same tint and style as the one Carlota wore tonight. She turned her girdle sideways so that its line might correspond with that in the painting, and rumpled her hair to make the resemblance more striking.

The old legend Assunta had told her recurred vividly tonight. She had been merely a girl princess, imprisoned in the old garden and towered castle by custom and precedent. And there had been a young fisherman from the village at the foot of the mountain, Peppino, who had come to the Castle. From her tower window she had seen and loved him, and at a fête in the village she had dared to escape over the wall and mingle with the people. Peppino had danced with her, and wooed her, not knowing she was the princess in disguise, and his sweetheart had stabbed her through jealousy. It was the tragedy of youth's eternal quest after romance and had lost nothing from Assunta's impassioned telling.

"Tonight, maybe," Carlota told herself, half laughingly, half in earnest, as she looked back in the mirror, "we scale the wall of Tittani."

CHAPTER IV

They passed up a carven, squarely built staircase to the second floor. The rooms were lofty and spacious. It seemed to Carlota, in the first glance about her, there here prevailed something of the same spirit that had marked her grandmother's receptions. Little groups gathered intimately in corners, a girl played something of Grieg's at the grand piano in the far room. Her hair had a golden sheen beneath the lampshade of Chinese embroidery, bronze and yellow.

The Marchese was in his happiest mood, the smiling courtier to his finger-tips. He left her with Mrs. Phelps, a little dark woman with frankly graying hair, but as the other guests came up the staircase, Carlota found herself on a low Moorish stool beside Carrollton Phelps's chair. He attracted her greatly. During the drive down the Avenue the Marchese had told her his story with unction. It was a favorite tale with him. Phelps had gone abroad in the earliest days of the war, joining the Lafayette Escadrille. Only those who knew him intimately before this happened, could appreciate what his personal gift of service had meant at that time even in the great summing-up of sacrifice that followed later. He had been a very successful artist, painting portraits of celebrities and social leaders. He had always been lavish in entertaining even then, and now, when he returned at thirty-five, a helpless paralytic from his final fall, the most amazing thing had been, as the Marchese expressed it, that "his wings were unbroken."

To Carlota, even the expression of his face brought a certain sense of encouragement, as if he divined the strangeness that she felt among all these new faces. His dark hair was prematurely whitened like his wife's, but she liked his lean, virile face, and keen, dark eyes. Even while his friends came and went beside him, he kept her there, asking her questions of her life in Italy.

"The Marchese has told me who you are—a glorious heritage. Mind you keep the pace, but don't let them starve you." His thin, strong hands gesticulated eagerly. "I know them. It was the same with me before I went over, success and more success and then—husks. Do you know the greatest thing that came to me from it all? My wife. We were married just before I left, and she went also, down in Serbia, where it was hell, you remember, nursing. I did not see her for four years, then her face came out of a gray cloud in a London hospital and I found the strength to live even to look at her. Don't let them deceive you, my dear. There is nothing at all in this thing called life but love and ideals. Will you tell that fellow to come here, the one with the violin."

The man stood by the piano, smiling at something the girl had just said as she turned from the keyboard. He bowed as Carlota gave her message, looked at her with his quizzical, half-closed eyes near-sightedly, and strolled to Phelps's side. Presently he returned.

"I have to bring you back. He only wanted me to meet you."

"I have been preaching your song of life," Phelps said, drawing himself up in his chair with the quick, restless movement that spoke of pain-cramped muscles. "This is the spirit of Serbia and all burdened peoples, Dmitri Kavec. Betty saved his life, and he has retaliated by keeping me in a ferment of enthusiasm over his country in her birth-pangs. He is not as sardonic as he appears. It is a pose."

Dmitri's face flushed, a shy deepening in color like an embarrassed boy.

"I never pose, Miss Trelango. My life is nothing, understand. I drop it overboard anywhere at all, but I had forgotten how to laugh or look at the sun, and Mrs. Phelps has shown it to me again, that is all. For her sake I put up with the abuse from this person here. Do you live down here?"

Carlota shook her head. Some one had taken the place of the girl at the piano, she could not see whom, but at the first low, minor chords, she was aware of a strange thrill of interest. Dmitri leaned back in the winged armchair next to Phelps and closed his eyes.

"Now we have some dream pictures," he said softly.

Carlota lifted her head eagerly to catch a glimpse of the player. The other men in the studio, even Phelps himself, had all seemed to her like the Marchese and Jacobelli, middle-aged, sophisticated, impervious to romance or sentiment, tired of all emotion. But the boy at the piano was different. He seemed to have forgotten the people around him, and yet he led their fancy where he would with the magic of his melody and tone pictures.

Looking from face to face Carlota saw the spell steal over each. The Marchese smiled with half-closed eyes, living over the joyous indiscretions of his youth. Mrs. Phelps had forgotten her guests as she bent over Carrollton, her fingers clasped in his with mothering tenderness. The girl who had played Grieg leaned back her head, her eyes filled with moody unrest. Dmitri bent forward, his cigarette burning itself to a neglected ash, a little smile on his lips. Almost imperceptibly his eyes watched Carlota.

A strange troubled feeling stole over her. It was as if the music had seized upon her own secret yearnings and was expressing them in all its exotic cadence. Suddenly she caught the eyes of the musician watching her as he played. The studio was dimly lighted from long, pendent temple lamps. The shifting glow from a tall candelabra on the piano showed her his face. It was young, with strong, lean lines, restless, seeking eyes, the chin and mouth lacking the sensuous weakness of the usual virtuoso. When he finished he crossed to her, pausing to answer a few who stopped him on the way. Dmitri sighed heavily and rose.

"See now, he will come and tell you he has been waiting for æons to see your face. He is all on fire. Do not extinguish the flame. He will tread the star path in this mood if you do not pitch him down to earth."

Carlota drew back from his amused eyes, behind a tall Moorish screen of carved olive fretwork. Why did they all smile at things that were sacred and beyond all sense of touch or sound? If the Marchese would only come near, she would beg him to leave now, now while it was all clear and fresh in her mind, the haunting, hurting sweetness of the music and the long look between them. And as she found her breath, he stood beside her. For the moment they were as isolated as if he had found her alone in some glade of Fontainebleau, like Pierrot and Columbine.

"Why did you try to hide from me?" His tone was low and broken with embarrassment. "I played to you—you knew that, didn't you? I tried to get to you before, but Dmitri had you. Who are you, you pagan girl with the wonder eyes? Tell me how you slipped in here tonight. Where I come from, we have gorgeous night moths; I love them, brown and tawny. Your eyes are that color, and your face is like a jasmine lifted to the moon. A warm, amber moon in late August, don't you know. You'll think I'm a crazy poet if I keep on, but it's your own fault. You make me want to be a poet and everything else that means adoration of you. Can't you speak to me?"

She closed her eyes as he gripped her hands in his. It was all so strange, so wrong, she knew how Maria would banish any such mad emotions, and yet she gloried in the tumult in her heart, in the swift response to every word he uttered, the reckless urge within her to turn to him. She strove to conquer it, and answer with composure.

"I think it is dangerous to speak so. Let us go to Mr. Phelps."

"And your eyes say all the while, 'I have found you,'" he laughed and took the seat beside her. "That's what I told myself when you looked at me. I've found her. Tell me, truthfully, aren't you glad to see me, aren't you?"

Carlota smiled up at him teasingly.

"The man you call Dmitri told me you would say this to me. You should not let him spoil the surprise."

"Did he? I didn't think the old gray fra had such discernment. Did he tell you my name? I know yours. It is all the sweethearts of the ages in one. That last thing I played was a Celtic love song; I saw you in a silver mist with the sea behind you and headlands and a girl moon clambering up the stairway of desire." He stopped short, eyeing her with boyish curiosity. "I wonder just who you are really. You came with old Veracci, didn't you?"

"I am Italian," Carlota answered gravely. "I have been here nearly three years. I am a singer."

"Are you?" he exclaimed eagerly. "That's why everything in me called out to you. I was in college, the third year, when the war came over here. I had wanted to go with Carrollton, but I was just eighteen then, so I promised my mother I'd wait. She'll love you," he added ingenuously. "I went over the next spring and came through all right; that's how I met Dmitri. We were all wounded about the same time."

"I thought you said you were all right?"

"I mean I didn't get killed or anything like that. Isn't Phelps a wonder? He'd give a dying coyote courage to howl. He told me to stick it out down here. I'm a composer. One of those kinks of fate put me into a perfectly respectable, sane Colorado family. Father was head of some smelter works out there. He started me through Columbia, with a postgrad. in law ahead of me, but I met Carrollton and he heard me play. Now I'm here until I make good."

"You will be famous." Carlota's eyes shone as she looked up at him. "Never have I heard such music, and I have listened to—" She checked herself, a sudden spirit of mischief prompting her. Was he not Pierrot, poor and struggling, with his heart a chalice of faith uplifted to the stars, while she was a child of fortune with the pathway to success fair and broad before her as the sea road to the Campagna back home. But for tonight, only tonight, she would be Columbine for him, straying, friendless Columbine, seeking shelter from the storm. "Some day I hope to be a great singer," she said softly.

"Do you? You beautiful, dreaming moth girl. And lessons cost like the very devil here in New York." He ran his fingers through his close-cut blond hair doubtfully, Carlota watching him shyly, thinking how much his profile was like that of a certain young emperor's on an old Roman coin she had. There was the same straight line from forehead to nostril, the same touch of youth's arrogance in his curving lips and cleft, projecting chin. "Do you know," he continued confidently, "I am sure I can help you. I could start you on your lessons, you know. Don't refuse. I'd love to help you, to even think I was. I have a rocky old studio down on the Square; nothing like this; it's poverty's back door compared to it, but if you'll come there, I will help you."

"Oh, but it is impossible," Carlota exclaimed, rising hurriedly. "I never go anywhere alone, it is not the custom with my people. It is so very kind of you, but"—she met his eyes wistfully—"I do not even know your name."

"I am Griffeth Ames. Ask Veracci, he knows me, so does Phelps. Listen, if you won't come for your own sake, for God's pity, come for mine. I'm starving down here for just what you gave me tonight when I first looked into your eyes—inspiration. I must see you and talk to you about my work; I need you. Will you come?"

"The heavens would fall if I did," she laughed unsteadily, trying to draw her hands from his clasp.

"Let them crash, who cares?" he said. "You'll come to me, I know you will. I'll call to you with music till you hear."

CHAPTER V

Maria was still indisposed on the following day. She asked many questions about the evening before, who the guests had been, and which ones had impressed Carlota. Always her eyes sought the girl's, testing her answers.

"I should have been happier if you had been there, tanta," Carlota told her tenderly. "You're not worrying still, are you? Nobody carried me away."

Maria closed her eyes as if to shut out any telltale gleam they might have held.

"I blame myself whatever happens," she sighed dramatically. "I should never have shown you the jewels. The ancient Hindoos are perfectly right. They claim the evil spirits, when imprisoned in the earth, produced gold and gems to ensnare the souls of mankind, especially women. Ah, mia carina, I am growing old and careless. You have made no further engagements?"

"The Marchese did not ask me to go anywhere else." Carlota bent over a low jar of cyclamen, her face turned away.

"Assuredly not. I am an old fool. Do not speak of the jewels to anybody, not even Jacobelli. I must place them in a safety-deposit vault; not keep them here. And while I am ill, you will not walk through the Park to the studio. I prefer to have you ride always. Come here to me." She half raised herself as Carlota knelt beside the couch, and framed her face in her palms. "You must not think I am harsh, my dearest one, or trying to keep you from pleasures you should have. It will all come to you in richest measure later on. Now we must be careful of you. You understand it is only because of our great love for you, do you not?"

"I know, surely, I understand."

"Has no one ever spoken to you on your way to the studio?" Maria's voice trembled with eager insistence. "Have you ever imagined you were followed? No, no, of course not. Do not be frightened at all.

It is only Maria's old love of the extravagant, the dramatic situation," she laughed softly, sinking back. "But remember to ride always when you are alone, and speak to no one."

Wonderingly, guiltily, too, Carlota reassured her, but when she reached the street she looked about her that day, with the first caution she had ever felt since their arrival in New York. What could Maria have meant? They knew no one in the city who could possibly have had any sinister intent towards them, yet there had been a lurking, secret fear in the eyes of the old signora.

At the corner of Fifth Avenue she hailed a taxicab, and arriving at the studio pleaded a headache as an excuse for a short lesson. Jacobelli was in a trying mood. Over and over again he railed at her, telling her that after his months of training, she was not putting her whole heart and soul into her singing. And suddenly Carlota leaned her chin on her palms at the back of the old grand piano, and asked:

"I wonder, maestro, if I were poor and unknown, and came to you, would you give me lessons because you had faith in my voice?"

"Certainly not," exclaimed Jacobelli positively. "I could never give you enough to win you the highest fame. The teaching is not sufficient. The great artiste must have peace of mind. We do not exist upon air; not even a bird with a celestial voice like yours. No, my dear, I would have told you to forget your pride and do exactly as you have done. Secure the financial backing of a man like Ogden Ward. I worship art. It has always been my life, but I recognize, like a sensible man, that in the times we live in we artists must still seek the patron even as Angelo and Raphael did. The public is not strong enough to sustain us. It cannot sustain itself, what would you? Some day, when the world is all golden with peace and plenty and brotherhood, then the singer will be the beloved prophet once again, and we shall delight in all the milk and honey and oil and burnt offerings we require, without the commonplace formality of contracts." He laughed at her heartily, leaning over to pat her hands. "Come early tomorrow; Mr. Ward will be here."

She left the studio with a sense of suffocating rebellion. They were all the same, Jacobelli, Ward, even Maria. Only the gentle, chivalrous old Marchese warmed her faith with his tender, hopeful philosophy, and were not his friends like him, even Dmitri Kavec? What was it this group had seemed to find in the fields of scarlet poppies that lifted idealism and faith in humanity above the creed of success and individual self-seeking?

As she stepped from the old red-brick building, a Greek flower vender wheeled his pushcart to the curb. She looked over the brilliantly tinted asters and chrysanthemums longingly, but purchased merely a spray of autumn leaves and hurried to the corner where the Riverside autobuses passed on their way crosstown to the Avenue.

Following after her leisurely came the man who had picked up her gloves in the vestibule some nights before. It would have been difficult to guess his age or nationality. He was slender, undersized, yet with a strongly knit, athletic frame that told of military training. Swarthy-skinned, dark-haired, with the brilliant black eyes of the southern races, he seemed merely a boy until one saw the somber, detached experience in his expression and eyes. As Carlota, almost trembling at her own temerity, stepped into the interior of a Washington Square 'bus, he followed her, swinging lightly up the narrow, winding staircase to the top.

The number which Griffeth Ames had given her was on the south side of the Square near MacDougal Street. It was an old four-story brownstone building, the last of five of the same kind sitting back in small flagged yards from the sidewalk. The paint which had scaled from its iron portico and balconies merely imitated the stucco front which had crumbled off in large patches. There were many names written on soiled cards and slips of white paper above the rows of bells in the entrance, and among them she found his. Just within the dim hall a young Italian girl knelt on a marble-topped table, polishing the brass ornaments on the old oval hall mirror. She smiled down absently as Carlota asked the way.

"At the very top of the house. You have to knock hard or he won't hear you."

She climbed the three flights quickly. The door at the top was ajar. It was surprising to find such spaciousness here under the gabled roof. As she hesitated on the threshold, her swift glance noticed how he had tried to partition off his private life from his professional with burlap draperies. It must have been a bleak place once, but Ames had taken it and had performed all of the customary artistic marvels to conceal its barrenness. Draperies dipped in eastern dyes, that he had picked up in the Syrian quarter on Washington Street, softened the angles of corners. The unsightly wooden partitions and beams below the peaked ceiling had acquired under his deft touch a deep rare old oaken hue the Pre-Raphaelites might have rested under. On the exterior of the low door he had even placed a brass knocker, a real antique from a shop uptown. Nobody, as Dmitri often said, but Fame would ever recognize it, and she, the willful damosel, would never climb those three flights of stairs unless she came en masquerade as a lark to tantalize him.

There was no fire in the deep, black grate. The windows above the broad seats in the gable inglenooks were wide open. The view and the old grand piano that stood crosswise in the room compensated for all other lacks. Ames was visibly embarrassed at her unannounced descent upon his quarters. He sat at a large, plain table drawn up before the south light, coatless, collarless, his hair ruffled into a crest, and ashes everywhere within his arm's-length radius. Upon one corner of the table there dozed a large yellow tomcat, palpably a nomad.

"I hope I have not come too soon?" she asked hesitantly.

He swept a pile of magazines and papers from a chair for her, but she chose the high window-seat.

"It isn't that, only I meant to set the stage for you," he said ruefully. "I wouldn't have had you find me like this for anything. When Ptolemy and I are alone here working, we just run a bachelor shop, and forget there are any other beings in the world."

"Make it a dress rehearsal, then. I like it up here very much." She looked out at the Square, the vivid autumn foliage accentuating the red and gold of the foliage and the vari-colored dresses of the Italian children playing there. It looked like some reckless, impressionistic painting, worked out merely in effective, daring splashes of color laid on with a palette knife. From the windows of Maria's chosen abode uptown, one gazed down upon an indefinite row of closed, chill, characterless dwellings, with no gleam of color from street to street.

"I would like to live down here too," she said thoughtfully. "It is very different from anything I have seen in New York before."

Ames watched her with eager appreciation. Her glossy, luxuriant hair waved back from her low forehead into a loose knot at the nape of her neck. Her face held the elusive appeal of La Cigale's. The memory of the old painting occurred to him with its appealing beauty and he felt a sudden protective tenderness towards this waif of summer's idleness.

"It is lonely; that's the only thing about it," he said, coming near her. "If it wasn't for Dmitri and the Phelpses I'd throw up the game sometimes and go West to the smelter."

"The smelter; what is that?" she asked curiously.

"Where they separate the ore from the quartz, you know, the real from the slag."

"Slag?" she repeated slowly. "Like the crucible? I know what you mean. I think you are in it now, here, don't you?"

"Dmitri would love you for that," he exclaimed eagerly. "It's all he talks about, the inner meaning of things. Like the crucible, the winepress, anything you like that means the big fight where you either make good or go under. I hate to think it's just chance. Sometimes when we were over in France, you couldn't help feeling that it was hit or miss. No matter how clever you were or well trained, you might be killed by any chance fragment of shell that strayed your way. It sort of wiped out the old idea of the plan. Know what I mean?" He quoted slowly, half under his breath:

> *"Our times are in His hand,*
> *Who said, 'A whole I planned,*
> *See all, be not afraid.'"*

Then, turning quickly to the cat, he lit a cigarette.

"Ptolemy, she comes in here and demoralizes us, old man. I'm getting sentimental."

He sat down to the piano carelessly, striking low minor chords, and then, unlike Jacobelli, he slipped into the first protesting strains of the duet from "Bohème." There was an enthusiasm and impulsive buoyancy about him that inspired Carlota to sing even as she had not when she had stood before the great maestro, Ames carrying Rudolpho's answer.

"Look at me when you sing," he commanded, and she shook her head in confusion.

"Does she not look at the candle?" she asked. "I—I forget when I look at you."

But when she had finished, he was almost humble in his supreme gratitude to whatever fate had sent her to his lone garret. With boyish fervor and earnestness he told her the whole world lay at her feet if only he could find a way to teach her.

"I can show you only the first steps of the way, and your voice is so glorious now, so perfect. Who taught you how to use it?"

"Every one sings in Italy," Carlota said evasively. "Even the girls at the fountains and the boys when they go out in the fishing fleet. I took only a few lessons there."

Inwardly, she felt overjoyed at the success of her ruse, and agreed to come to him twice a week for lessons if he would accept in payment whatever she was able to give. But he would not listen to this.

"It's enough to have you as my pupil. When other people hear you sing and know that I have taught you, it will bring me all sorts of other work. I know. Besides, you inspire me. Yes, you do. I don't know what it is." He drew in a deep breath, watching her. "Guess we were just a couple of old lazy dubs here, weren't we, Ptolemy? I've wanted to work. It's all been here in my head, till I couldn't sleep nights with the themes rampant, but I couldn't catch them. They were like fireflies. Ever try to get them at night? I did when I was a little chap out West. I always wanted to train them. Must you go so soon? I didn't get your full name the other night. Carlota, the Marchese called you, didn't he?"

"Just call me that," she told him gravely. "I would not be allowed to come here if my people knew. They are very conservative."

"It doesn't matter, anyway," he said confidently. "You'll never use it in your work. I don't care just so long as you come. Dmitri said you never would. He walked down here last night with me. Queer chap, isn't he? Did you like him?"

"I didn't notice him," Carlota spoke thoughtfully, not realizing the purport of her own words as she looked up at him on the threshold of the stairs. "I only remembered you."

CHAPTER VI

The weeks following were filled with a romantic glamour for them both. Ames never realized how much his pupil was teaching him. After he had given her the benefit of what little knowledge he possessed, Carlota would coax him from the piano, and letting her own fingers stray over the keys, would suggest carelessly:

"Do you not like it better this way?"

He never suspected that she was giving him all of Jacobelli's tricks in teaching, all she knew of the great maestro's art of technique. He only knew that the fame of his pupil was spreading through the Quarter and that people were coming up the narrow stairs to inquire his rates as teacher of voice culture.

"If I can only get enough to keep the friendly wolf jolly and contented, I can find time to work on my opera," he told her happily. "I owe it all to you, though. You've got such a perfect voice naturally, you don't need a teacher, and here everybody who hears you sing will give me the credit for it."

Carlota smiled at him silently, delighted that her visits to the studio were bringing him even a glimmer of success. To her they were all that filled her days now with expectancy. Maria's ill health continued to prevent her from calling for Carlota every day at the uptown studio, and while she longed to tell the Marchese, she feared that even his solicitude might put an end to the only gleam of romance or adventure that had come to her. So far as she knew, no one had discovered her visits to the Square, yet never did she leave the arched doorway of her home that the nonchalant stranger did not follow her. Patiently, without haste or apparent malevolence, he shadowed her to Jacobelli's or downtown. Sometimes in the morning, he would lounge at Cecco's cigar store around the corner on Madison Avenue, smoking his endless store of curious, long, thin cigarettes. From Cecco's one could look through the middle of the block towards Fifth Avenue, over the tops of intervening fences. The only apartment house was the one where Maria Roma and Carlota lived. And while he chatted over the latest juggling with the fates of nations and peoples overseas, he would forget to look at Cecco rolling cigarettes, and eye the distant fire escapes like a bird of prey, gauging the flight.

One day, as she came from Ames's place, the impulse swept over Carlota to see the old Marchese and tell him. He would understand, she was sure, and she longed to have him know Griffeth well, to appreciate his work and help him.

Through Maria and Jacobelli she knew that even in New York, where the power of great wealth dominated the will of the people through its manifold channels of politics, society, and charity, yet there was an altar erected even here to the unknown god of truth, and the Marchese stood ever as a high priest of the eternal verities.

"You must not be discouraged, my dear," he had told her one afternoon at tea beside Maria's couch. "Look beneath the surface of things. The brass band is always at the head of the procession. Once one has escaped its clamor, one may pay attention to the motive behind the parade, yes? There is always in any race, in any period, a certain group of people, in all walks of life, who worship truth wherever manifest, in art or the grace of right living. It is absurd to claim that any class has a monopoly of this spirit. Ogden Ward is a multi-millionaire, doubtless a thorough robber baron in his way, yet he serves a certain purpose through his fascination for the beautiful and rarest in art. Some day, when, God willing, he passes on, perhaps his collections will be given back to the people. I can do little except encourage this spirit wherever I find it. Casanova, of the Opera, is a noble fellow, yet he must perforce kowtow when the mighty atoms on the subscribers' list say they will have this or that. But that does not prevent Casanova from his personal worship of real art, you see. I know him very well, indeed, and some day he will meet you."

Remembering this, Carlota stepped into a shop on Eighth Street and telephoned to the Lafayette. It was the one golden moment when she felt she must see the Marchese and tell him everything, take him back with her to the old studio and make him listen to Ames's compositions for the new opera. But at that particular instant the Marchese was meeting Ogden Ward at his club by appointment, and the message was left on a slip in his box at the hotel unheeded.

"I want you to meet Count Jurka; used to be with the Bulgarian Legation, remember. He has proven to be a very valuable agent along the new lines of readjustment. I met him in Egypt first in connection with the Rhodopis emeralds. They were found in the royal mummy, and there was some argument in connection with them. I had furnished the means for the research work and I have the emeralds. He is quite a savant in his way when it comes to the history of famous jewels."

"I do not care for them," returned the old Marchese blandly, as he ensconced himself in a deep leather armchair and smiled. "Relics of barbarism, my dear Ward; rings in noses and bangles on leaping toes, merely a variation of the same impulse in humanity to decorate itself that we see today in certain types of women."

"And men also. Say it." Ward leaned forward on the polished table and laid a small leather case before him. "I like to carry unset stones around in my pockets, not for decoration. What would you call me, Marchese?"

"An idolator, either of the beautiful or of the peculiar quality of concentrated value that seems to lie in jewels."

Ward lifted out two pearls, wrapped in tissue papers, and held them in the hollow of his palm.

"You're right. Here are the largest gems from the collections of the murdered Empress Elizabeth of Austria. They always darkened when she wore them. She had them dipped regularly in a perforated casket into the sea to restore the luster. It is not alone the value of them that interests me. I like stones that have tragic stories connected with them. There was a necklace of pearls around the throat of Marie Stuart as she was being led to execution. I have never been able to find them. Jurka is also a collector and lover of gems from the historic standpoint. He is standing by the desk now, the tall fellow, fair-haired. Do you recognize him?"

The Marchese looked through the arched doorway at the man Ward had designated. He was trying to place where he had seen him, and suddenly smiled, one forefinger at his forehead.

"He was at the Lafayette a week ago Saturday, dining with Palmieri, Collector of the Port, a delightful person."

"Well posted on the valuation of jewels," Ward remarked laconically. He paused to light his favorite pipe with the air of assured bonhomie he assumed when relaxed. "How is Carlota?"

"She progresses well."

"Why not after two years under Jacobelli? He tells me her technique is faultless, but she lacks temperament."

"He does not know her," the Marchese answered placidly. "The temperament is there dormant. It needs but the awakening. She is still a child."

"Her mother married before she was her age."

"And never sang at all. Waken the Paoli nature in a girl like Carlota and you will lose her. We do not wish her to experience love, to run the gamut of emotion—it is fatal to a woman of genius. Then, too, afterwards, you always reach her through the husband. Husbands of geniuses—ah, my dear Ward, I could tell you of many catastrophes."

"Not marriage." Ward knocked the tobacco from his coat sleeve that had fallen there while he had filled his pipe. "An affair possibly. A quick flurry of passion that might sweep over her like a clarifying fire, burning out the underbrush in her nature. You might arrange a quiet little dinner at my apartment with Signora Roma and Carlota. I do not think I have heard her sing lately."

He rose at the approach of Count Jurka and presented him. The old Marchese was genial and full of welcome. Had he not seen him already down in the haunt of the selective with Palmieri?

"I did not see you there." Jurka spoke with a very clear, careful enunciation, his large blue eyes never winking as he met the other's pleased scrutiny. "Palmieri is interested in some fête for Italian child sufferers of the war—very worthy object. I wished him to meet Mrs. Carrington Nevins, who has been most helpful to me in organizing committees for my own stricken land."

As they sat down Ward began without preamble, his fingers pressing nervously on the small leather case containing the pearls.

"I told Jurka I thought you could assist him. He is gathering data on rubies. Do you know of one called the Zarathustra? It is a perfect pigeon blood, second to the largest in the world."

"I am absolutely ignorant concerning jewels," smiled the Marchese indulgently. "Consider me a perverted mind."

Jurka leaned slightly towards him.

"I have already traced it to Italy, but many years ago. It was part of a collection, rubies and pearls. I thought it might have come over here and been disposed of to Mr. Ward. It is almost impossible now to find out what has become of most royal jewels, I mean the historic ones. Sooner or later, I have understood, if their tale of tragedy is terrible enough, they find their way here."

Ward did not pick up the opening. Sauntering away from the club up the Avenue, the Marchese pondered later, not upon the Zarathustra ruby, but on Ward's invitation. At first he hesitated at a crossing, wishing he might talk it over with Maria, but finally contenting himself with telephoning to her. Carlota caught the rising inflection of exultation as Maria accepted for them both.

"Certainly I'm well enough to go," she cried; then, hanging up the receiver, "Ah, beloved child, you do not understand the conquest you have made already. But it will not do to appear too eager. You must learn to act like your grandmother, distant, gracious, always the queen."

But Carlota was supremely indifferent to the favor shown her by Ward. For weeks she had been full of strange, gay little moods and sudden, tempestuous caresses that left Maria breathless and speculative. She smiled over her shoulder now, brushing her long dark curls before the Venetian mirror.

"Surely, bella mia"—Signora Roma spoke with emphasis—"surely you comprehend what this means to your progress. There are yet two years before you, possibly more, before you make your début. Therefore, you must be diplomatic and save your independence until you are assured that the race is won. You must appear perfect at Mr. Ward's dinner. I will dress you like the starlight, like the pearl from the sea, très ingénue, so he will see the great sensation you will make."

Carlota laughed teasingly.

"I would love to make my début in some splendid barbaric opera, where I could wear cloth of gold and armlets, bangles. I wish I could sing Semiramide at the very beginning, or Fedora, and you, you adorable old tanta, will probably persuade Jacobelli to make me bow as Juliette or Marguerite."

"The Veronese are very dark like you, and, thank God, you will still be slender and maiden-like," sighed Maria reflectively. "It is a wonderful opportunity to impress Mr. Ward. You had better effect Juliette that night."

"I don't like this thing you call opportunity. I like, as the Marchese says, what is to be will be. I like the inevitable. It must have been delightful to feel your destiny was written in the stars." She pinned her hair up carelessly. "Mr. Ward is the only person from whom we have been compelled to borrow money. He will be repaid amply—in money."

"Only a person who could appreciate the priceless value of such a voice as yours could have had such faith. He is the greatest patron of the arts in the world—"

"I hate patronage. It simply means that he can pay the highest price for what he desires, that is all." Carlota turned to her stormily.

"Another may have a million times more appreciation, more love, more yearning to aid, and still stand with hands bound because he has no money. I hate patronage. I would rather sell every jewel in your treasure chests than give a man like Ogden Ward the right to order my appearance at his dinner."

At Maria's gesture of despair her mood changed instantly to one of coaxing tenderness. To please her only would she go, not because Ward wished her to. She had hurried home after telephoning the Marchese, and his message had come when she had felt most rebellious. It had become increasingly difficult for her to get away for her lessons with Ames twice a week. Today Signora Roma had been more curious than ever, and it had taken the most elusive of excuses to soothe her. All manner she had made up so far, little necessary trips to the art shops, the galleries, the quiet cathedral, feeling that she was indeed playing Columbine in the garret studio down on the Square. Yet she was almost forced to attend a dinner given by Ward as if it were an honor bestowed by him. This they would urge her to do, Maria, Jacobelli, and even the Marchese; yet, if they knew of her visits to Ames, she would be compelled to stop them because they were unconventional.

Almost in a spirit of audacious bravado, she deliberately started for the studio the following morning. It would be a surprise to Ames, and she wanted to talk over the dinner with him. For the first time in weeks the watching figure was absent from its customary post near Cecco's store. When she left the 'bus, it seemed as if she could have lifted her whole heart to the Quarter in relief. It was like some enchanted realm to her where hopes and dreams were tangible, and only facts untrue. Spring stood tiptoe on the Arch and scattered her soul-disturbing germs abroad. She knelt at the edge of the old fountain and mimed at herself in the water that had just been permitted to splash therein from the far-off springs of Askohan quite as if they had flowed from Castalian founts. She flirted with the rainbow that hangs over the leaping spray on sunny mornings, and wigwagged joyous discontent to every possible shepherd in the distance.

From a flower-stand at the corner Carlota recklessly bought daffodils and narcissus. They had grown in phalanxes along the wall of Tittani. Almost she had decided to tell Maria and Jacobelli she would never go to the dinner, never accept any more aid from Mr. Ward, when suddenly she was arrested by the sight of a dark gray limousine standing at the curb in front of Ames's residence. Clinging around it was a flock of little Italian children, trying to peer into the interior sanctum, a study in suède leather with dark red Jacqueminot roses in slender French gray silver vases in each corner.

She hesitated outside the studio door. A clear, well-modulated voice came from within, a woman's voice.

"Twice a week, then, Mr. Ames, and we will not speak of terms. I have heard of your wonderful success with beginners, and Nathalie's temperament requires an environment like this, unusual and bizarre, don't you know? It wilts at any touch of the customary or mediocre that you find in most musical studios uptown. Here you fairly radiate atmosphere."

She hesitated just as Ames opened the door. He looked flushed and elated, and seized her hand to present her to his callers.

"Oh, but we have already heard of you, Miss—er—Carlota!" Mrs. Carrington Nevins exclaimed. "This must be your little Italian pupil who sings so charmingly, Mr. Ames. Chandos told us all about you at his tea last week, how you came and went like a little flitting city sparrow, and not even Mr. Ames knew your real name."

Carlota stood in silence, her chin lifted, her long lashes downcast as she drew off her gloves slowly. The daffodils and narcissus lay in the curve of her arm. She caught a little smile on the face of the girl standing with Ames, this tall, fair girl with the ice-blue eyes, and a wave of fiery scorn swept over her at this invasion of her own particular haunt, Columbine's special chimney-pot.

"You must hear her sing," Ames said positively, going to the piano. "Lay off your things, Carlota. I want you just to try that little barcarolle you taught me."

"I cannot sing today, Mr. Ames." Carlota met his surprised eyes serenely. "It is impossible."

"But just this one—" He stopped abruptly, warned by the expression of her face.

Mrs. Carrington Nevins raised her lorgnette, the slenderest excuse for one in carven tortoise shell and platinum, gazing at the girl amusedly.

"My dear, I believe you are temperamental like all singers should be. It is your prerogative. But you must remember all that Mr. Ames is doing for you, and try to obey him. Isn't she a dear little thing, Nathalie?"

"Do you live right down here in the Sicilian quarter?" asked Nathalie eagerly. "It's so funny. I made mother drive through there today and the car made quite a sensation."

Carlota turned her head and looked at her in a haughty, detached way.

"I have never been there. I am a Roman."

CHAPTER VII

Carlota stood aside to let them pass down the narrow stairs. In the half light from the dusty skylight overhead she seemed like a shadow excepting for the light in her eyes. The sunlight from the studio's south window sent a lane of gold through the open door, and she watched Nathalie as she laid her hand in Ames's lingeringly.

"I shall love it here," she heard her say, in her rather plaintive, appealing way. "And I want you to be sure and stay for dinner Tuesday. You can suggest things for our Italian fête next month, can't he, mother?"

"I shall be delighted if I can be of any service," Ames told her, as he followed down the four flights of stairs to the waiting car.

Even Ptolemy seemed to catch the contagion of trouble in the air and leaped stealthily out of her way to the top of the piano. Carlota waited, standing in the center of the floor, her eyes ablaze with scorn as Ames entered.

"You were exactly like old Pietro, my grandmother's courier," she told him. "I have never seen you like that before. Who are these people? Why did you ask me to sing for them?"

He swept her a low bow jubilantly.

"Dear, it means ten dollars a lesson. That is the Mrs. Carrington Nevins and her only daughter. She will bring me other pupils, too, from her crowd out on the north shore. You're my mascot."

"Did you try her voice?" She spoke very softly. "Do you intend giving her lessons?"

"I certainly do." He began rummaging in the wall cupboard after his stock of china. "We're going to celebrate my first real success. I'm going to the market and buy a spread and telephone Dmitri to come down, and you shall preside and sing."

"Did you try her voice?" demanded Carlota again, her voice a warning of smouldering anger.

He nodded his head happily. "She has a very appealing quality, a light lyric soprano, well pitched and true. Of course she has had a lot of training."

Carlota deliberately swept a jar of golden tulips from the top of the piano to the floor in crashing fragments. She herself had bought the jar for him, a squat plaster one, painted in dull-gold and Tuscan fruit tints. It had been her whim to keep it filled with flowers. There had been a small urn like it before a statue of Daphne in the garden at Tittani, and she had always as a child kept fresh flowers there, she told him. Now, it lay like a symbol of broken faith at her feet. As Ames swung about in amazement, she drew on her gloves with superb indifference.

"Will you kindly tell me the meaning of this?" he demanded hotly.

"It means—nothing, signor, nothing at all. I have an engagement today. I cannot take my lesson from you."

But he saw the trouble and pain in her eyes instantly and caught her hands in his.

"Now, listen, Carlota, you know all this means to me—to us. They would never have come at all if it hadn't been for you. You heard what she said. Chandos is the English painter downstairs. He's heard you sing and has told them about it."

Slowly the tears gathered heavily to her lashes. She had given him the full benefit of all she had learned from the great Jacobelli, and now he would give it to this girl for a few paltry dollars.

"Why do you have to take her when she has everything? Go down through the Quarter and find some poor singer. Take even the children. But give it freely, not for money. I cannot bear to see you acting like old Pietro before such people. Grateful? Do you think that Jacobelli was ever grateful in his life?"

"What do you know about Signor Jacobelli?" he demanded teasingly. "You're angry because she called you a city sparrow, my nightingale, and you're right, but I can't afford to turn down such a chance. I've got to live here if I am to work on my opera and succeed, and this is enough for me."

"You may do as you like, but I shall not come here as long as that girl takes lessons from you."

"But can't you see how it will benefit us both?" He stopped before her impatiently. "You are my star pupil. Perhaps I might even persuade Mrs. Nevins to let you sing at one of her musicales. If I could get her interested in my opera, think what it would mean for me, dear—"

"I did not think you were of the kind who seek patronage," she said slowly. "I will not come again. Not for one instant would I sing for that woman. You have no ideals. I believed you were altogether different."

"Carlota, come back," he called after her; but the door shut with a slam that sent Ptolemy scurrying for cover, and he stopped short, frowning with a quick, boyish resentment at her suspicion of him. Although there had never been a definite declaration of love between them, yet their whole acquaintance had ripened in an atmosphere of romantic glamour, a piquant, elusive mutual acceptance of each other idealized. He could not have understood the surging resentment in Carlota's heart as she went uptown to take her real lesson from Jacobelli. Once in the Square she had tossed the jonquils and daffodils broadcast to the children around the fountain. Her mind was a tumult of emotions, of hot rebellion against Ames's acceptance of her coming as a gift of Fate that was his due. She knew her identity was a mystery to him. He had told her of asking Phelps, and being told she was a protégée of the Marchese Veracci a young Italian singer in whom he was interested; that was all.

He had all of the artist's selfish point of view, she thought. He had not even caught the personal side of her anger. He saw merely the professional jealousy of one singer towards another in her antagonism towards Nathalie Nevins, and this attitude added fuel to Carlota's raging indignation against him. He could not even grasp or understand all that the visits had meant to her, all that she had given him gladly. He had not even been musician enough to distinguish between the quality of her voice and that of Nathalie. And suddenly it flashed across her that possibly Jacobelli was right; that she did lack power and dramatic force, feeling, passion, all that made the really great singer.

When she reached the studio she flung the outer door wide even as Maria might have done. Signor Jacobelli was at the piano amusing himself. The taunting, passionate notes of the *Habanera* crashed upon her as she stood a moment transformed utterly from the somber, unawakened girl he had last met. And in an instant she had picked up the melody, provocative, imperative, daring, sauntering into the room with all of Carmen's tricks at her finger-tips, at her tongue's end. Jacobelli turned quickly, catching the new note of passion and power. She did not appear even to see him, but flung her whole soul into the song and the underlying tragedy of its motif.

"Brava!" murmured the old maestro, huskily. "Try now the *Dance of the Tambourines*."

As she finished the gypsy song, he sprang from the bench, kissing her hands in ecstasy.

"I do not know, I do not ask from whence this has come to you, but I thank God it is there at last, the divine note for which I have prayed. So you shall sing for Mr. Ward at his dinner, ma bella, and take him by storm."

Carlota's eyes glowed with anger as she threw aside her cloak and hat. She looked for the instant like a reincarnation of the youthful Paoli, as he remembered her back at La Scala.

"I will not sing for him or be shown off to him any more," she told him hotly. "I detest him and all people like him."

Jacobelli threw back his head, laughing delightedly.

"Aha! Temper?" he cried. "It is the beginning of temperament, thanks be to God. We expect it, my dear, sooner or later. The artistic temperament is like the resistless forces of nature, the storm, the volcano, the tidal wave, the lightning. Life would be tame without them in spite of the danger, would it not? We crave the thrill. Never have I heard the great dramatic quality before in your voice. Ah, you shall sing all the glorious colorful rôles they have had to shelve because there was no one to sing them."

Carlota had turned from him and gone to the west windows, the tears blinding her sight. Even the agony of one's heart, then, had a commercial value. Life was merely the arena where one gave all for applause, where human emotions merely added to the thrill of suspense. The deeper the reality of the knife-thrust, the cleverer the counterfeit acting.

"I hate it all," she sobbed brokenly. "I wish we could go back to Tittani. Tell them my voice is hopeless, maestro, and let me go."

Jacobelli lit a cigarette deliberately, eyeing her thoughtfully. He tipped a chair backwards and seated himself, rocking slowly on two of its legs.

"Who is he?" he asked gently.

Carlota looked back at him in angry silence, startled into caution at his words, but he waved one plump hand at her airily and reassuringly.

"Remember, my child, I have known both your mother and grandmother. History moves in recurrent cycles, even the history of human hearts, and particularly when we consider heredity. I talked with Margherita Paoli when first she took Bianca from the convent. She told me her theory of life for a woman of genius and I agreed with her perfectly. Love in its perfection is the supreme sacrifice of self, art is the elevation of self, the crowning of self. They are at war eternally. So I told her, and she said she would keep Bianca safe behind the wall of Tittani while she studied. Never should the danger of love approach her until her success was assured, and this creed was impressed upon your mother, my dear, with what result? Even while we two fools prated, she was listening in the garden to the boy Peppino and was gone before her mother even guessed their love."

Carlota turned back into the room suddenly, her eyes brilliant with eager appeal.

"Tell me who John Tennant was?" she asked him. "Why did my nurse use to tell me that no woman could escape over the wall of Tittani without meeting the tragic fate of the Princess Fiametta? Oh, you are all so blind! You treat me like a baby, and never think I hear or see anything. Don't you suppose I ever think or reason? I used to go down to the end of the garden looking seaward, to that little stone house where they told me he had lived and died. Once I went in when I found the door unlocked. Everything was just as he had left it, and while I was wondering what it all meant, my grandmother came in from the little walk along the terrace above and I knew she had been weeping. Then Maria told me only his name. Who was he?"

Jacobelli made a magnificent gesture.

"I may not tell you. The secret of his being there was only known to his friend Wallace, the Marchese, and myself. I found out by accident when I sought her and implored her to return to the stage. She loved him, and he never even knew that she was near him in the garden or that it was her love and bounty he lived upon. Ah, the wonderful woman she was! Only as he died, unconscious in her arms, could she speak to him or caress him, and he never knew. Think of her pride, imperial in its abnegation."

"But my mother was happier."

He shrugged his shoulders.

"Who can say? Women are complex. Bianca was all tenderness, a flower of love. She did not pass the walls to seek adventure, but to escape from ambition. When I first met her fresh from La Pietà and heard your grandmother's plans, I thought, never, never, with such eyes and lips. And I told her the lines from *Romeo et Juliette*; you know them?

> *"'With love's light wing did I o'erperch these walls,*
> *For stony limits cannot hold love out.'"*

"I am glad she escaped!" flamed back Carlota. "Even my grandmother, who knew in her own heart that love was all to a woman, would have shut her own child away from its beauty and truth—"

"From its agony and devastating influence," Jacobelli protested placidly. "To the woman of genius this is so, my dear. You cannot discuss it logically because you have never experienced love. Even I have never loved to distraction, always with reason, and I have been most happy. I have buried two beautiful, gifted women who adored me."

Carlota turned suddenly away, afraid of the flood of words on her lips that she longed to pour out. It would only arouse suspicion against her if she went too far, and already the reaction was setting in, and she felt a great weariness of body and spirit. Were they not right, after all, she thought, as she stood by the window looking riverward? Somewhere she had read that the yearning after ideals was merely the soul's subconscious memory of another life. Was it then foolish to seek a path to the stars through the world of everyday selfishness and commercialism? Griffeth accepted patronage gladly for the sake of his operetta. She would have had him finish it in the high seclusion of the garret studio and win recognition and fame as his right once it had been submitted to the directors of the Opera. Instead he must seek the favor of persons like Mrs. Nevins, must add the weight of their influence before the magic doors would open to him. And in order to win Mrs. Nevins's interest and friendship, he must give lessons to her daughter and constantly flatter and compromise with his own critical faculty.

She who loved directness and clarity of vision and the straight, white road ahead, faced suddenly the devious, twisting path that led to success and popularity. Yet there never was a straight road that led to a mountain peak, she thought. Always the winding way, the compromise with risk and danger until one reached the summit of desire. She smiled slowly, and turned to Jacobelli, smoking in long, leisurely puffs until she should have changed her mind.

"I will go to Mr. Ward's dinner and sing for him," she said.

He laid aside his pipe.

"The caprice and passion of the woman always move in a circle. Wait but patiently, and behold, she is back at the starting-point, and is willing. My dear, you show common sense and astuteness. Forget all this love nonsense. I know not what had roused you, but put it away from you. Ogden Ward can open every door for you in the operatic world. I would not be too indifferent and petulant with him. Ah, if I could only teach you your grandmother's queenly way, the mingling of alluring charm and condescension, the aloofness of her favor—"

Carlota drew on her gloves, watching him the while.

"I may toss roses from the top of the wall; that is it, signor?" she said gravely. "I shall try to remember."

CHAPTER VIII

Ward had handed over the details of the dinner to his Japanese butler, Ishigaki, who presided over the town house of the millionaire.

In spite of her dislike of him and reluctance to accept favors, Carlota felt a thrill of almost childish excitement over the novelty of it all as she entered the upper salon which had been turned into a private banqueting-hall for the occasion.

The walls were hung with dull-gold, Oriental draperies, weighted down with embroidery. A glow from hidden shaded lights left the room in a twilight haze of amethyst and saffron. The air was fragrant with faint, strange perfumes. Brazier lamps burned somberly in stone lanterns half revealed behind red and gold lacquered screens. On the surface of a pool sunken in the center of the teakwood dining-table, half-opened lotus buds floated, and curious, iridescent-plumaged waterfowl stood amongst them, dazed and hesitating, goldfish darting at their feet, and tiny turtles scrambling aimlessly up the sides of the pool.

"I hoped it might amuse you," Ward said when he found Carlota bending over the table in delight. He had never seen her in evening dress before, and Maria had spared no pains or thought for this that might be her night of conquest.

"You shall be Juliette in her triumph," the old singer had said. "Cloth of silver with a veil of lace from the Colonna wedding chests. And the very cap of seed pearls which your grandmother bought from the old antique dealer in Verona near the bridge as you leave the palace. And just a girdle of filigree silver, set in pearls with tassels of them. But for your throat, nothing at all. It is encircled by beauty quite enough. First I thought to let you wear her chain of rubies with the black cross. Then the necklace of opals. She loved them. It came from Russia and was part of the great Catherine's treasure. One of the Orloffs gave it to Paoli. I would not have you wear anything tonight that might bring the evil eye upon you."

Carlota had laughed at her earnest insistence. She felt no interest in Ward himself, only a deep-rooted resentment against the circumstances which forced her to accept his hospitality when she disliked him. Even now she merely smiled at his words, and turned eagerly to greet the old Marchese. The latter's gray eyebrows arched with approval when he beheld the result of Maria's costuming.

"So soon you grow into your kingdom, mia carina," he exclaimed half teasingly, half musingly. "Behold, yesterday, Mr. Ward, it was a child whom I cajoled with chocolate almonds. I do assure you, she was the utter gourmand for them, rummaging into my pockets like a squirrel, and now we bow to her sovereignty, is it not so?"

"The bloom fulfills the promise of the bud," Ward answered gravely, and Carlota's eyes held a startled wonderment as he gazed down at her. It seemed tonight as if his glance even held a covert challenge that aroused every element of resentment in her nature. Throughout the dinner she was reticent and unresponsive. The Marchese, as always, was so absorbed in his little anecdotes and sallies of wit that Ward's attentions escaped him. Maria observed, but gave no sign of annoyance; rather, she was filled with pride at the influence of her beloved child over so great a man as Ward. Jacobelli ate and drank as a connoisseur, paying little attention to the conversation about him, but relaxing under the mellowing influence of Ward's wines and Ishigaki's solicitous ministrations. Finally he caught Carlota's refusal to sing as her host urged her after they rose from dinner.

"It is no time tonight to show caprice, cara mia," he exclaimed pompously. "Come, I would have you sing and prove to Mr. Ward how soon you will triumph at the Opera."

Carlota's eyes sought the Marchese's in swift appeal, but he merely nodded to her encouragingly above the lifted rim of his glass of old Amontillado.

"Miss Trelango is only afraid that you will put her through your professional paces, Jacobelli," Ward interposed easily. "Show the Marchese and Signora Roma those new photographs in the east gallery of the excavations at Rhodopis. You will find the emeralds we took from the royal mummies there also. Ishigaki will open the case for you."

Jacobelli smiled understandingly, and led the way. The Japanese moved noiselessly about the salon, turning off a light here and there until only those in the stone lanterns gave a nebulous glow. When they were alone, Ward moved one of the lacquered screens from its place, disclosing a tall panel of solid gold embroidery set in ebony. Flamingoes moved through sunlit marshes.

"This will amuse you," he said, stepping upon a convex spring set in the floor. The panel slipped silently up. "This is my favorite music-room." He led the way through the narrow door into the interior. It was domed with stained glass, a fan fretwork above the Empire grand piano assuring perfect acoustics. The walls were in flat dull gold, with peacocks and gray apes in conventionalized designs, hand-painted. A rock crystal vase held irises, gold and purple. The light filtered cunningly through the stained glass in rays of twilight splendor. "I have kept this room for you the first time you should sing to me alone."

Carlota closed her eyes as she seated herself at the piano, the memory of the little garret studio of Ames a vivid, poignant hurt to her pride. He to whom she had given all her faith and love, and he had held it so lightly, where to this man no effort was too great to win her favor.

"Jacobelli tells me you have gained. Sing what you love best yourself."

And instead of choosing some grand-opera aria, she sang "O Sole Mio," as she had learned it from Ames. Over their lunches in the studio, he would sing it to her, lunches of bread and fruit and salad, glorified by love and song. Out in the east gallery Jacobelli caught the air and frowned, but the Marchese inclined his head to listen contentedly. As the last notes ended, Ward bent over her suddenly, his arms around her, his lips seeking hers dominantly. Crushed in his powerful embrace, she strove to free herself, but Ward had waited two years for this moment, and she felt her strength leave her as he held her. The crystal vase crashed behind him as he tripped backwards over the slender stand, her hand holding his face from her.

"Maria!" she called. "Maria! Come to me!"

"Let her alone," warned Jacobelli, placing himself at the door of the gallery. "She must learn poise and command of herself."

Maria glared at him, infuriated.

"Mother of God, when the child needs me!" she cried, and sped along the salon to the inner room. The Marchese's glance met that of the maestro with troubled questioning.

"Surely, he would not attempt anything to alarm her. You do not think—" The old Italian spread out his stout, expressive hands.

"I do not think when I am with such a man as Ogden Ward. He is a law to himself."

Veracci's expression changed instantly. From the easy, genial old diplomat there seemed to fall over his face the mask of the soldier.

"No man is that," he answered. "I would hold him accountable if he has annoyed the child."

Before Maria had reached them, Carlota had released herself. She turned to him with clenched hands, her face white with anger.

"Take me home, tanta!" she exclaimed. "I—I am not well."

Ward regarded them both with amused speculation.

"You are temperamental, my dear, perhaps a trifle gauche also, too much the gamine in your play." He held out one hand to show the scratch that ran like a scarlet thread along the skin. "Tell Jacobelli I say it is time to prepare for her début."

Carlota stood with her back to the piano, her eyes filled with quick tears, Maria's caressing hand on her arm to check her.

"I do not need your permission," she said passionately. "I have the voice and I will go to Casanova myself, and tell him who I am. He will hear me. And I will pay you back everything. You do not know that I can easily. I have my grandmother's jewels—"

"But, my poor foolish one," cried Maria, "Casanova would not give you standing-room in his chorus if you went to him without the backing of money and patronage."

"Then I will go back to Italy. Where is the Marchese, Maria?" She spoke with sudden quietness and dignity. "I am sorry, Mr. Ward. Doubtless the fault is mine. I do not seem to have learned my part according to the rôle expected of me."

Ward bowed as she passed him, his own face tense with repression. Out in the long gallery Jacobelli waited, detaining the Marchese over the collection of emeralds. Carlota pleaded a sudden faintness to account for her departure and he accompanied them down to Jacobelli's waiting car, returning for a final glass of his favorite cordial in Ward's library.

"You are not only the art lover supreme," the old gentleman said genially, ensconcing himself in a deep armchair, "but likewise you know how to select the rare, the unusual. Before I had the enjoyment of our personal acquaintance, I had heard of you as an eccentric, that you carried about in your pockets loose pearls worth thousands, merely to touch and gaze on them when you were in the critical moment of some great financial deal. Is it so?"

Ward smiled non-committally.

"I have collected pearls amongst other things."

"Then perhaps you noticed the cap our sweet protégée wore tonight, the Juliette mode, a network of pearls? That is a bit of very delicate craftsmanship, sixteenth-century work. Margherita Paoli's collection was thought marvelous in her day. Every piece has its own history. She left it intact for Carlota."

"Where is it?" The unwinking, light gray eyes of the financier watched every shade of expression on his guest's face.

"I was not in the confidence of the Contessa," responded the Marchese suavely, almost regretfully, as he touched the ash from his cigarette tip and watched it fall on the curled leaf of gold repoussé.

Carlota leaned her head back on the suède cushion in Jacobelli's car, gazing out at the Avenue's lights as they flashed by. It had been raining, and they glowed through the wet glass in prismatic hues like in a spectrum. Maria's arm was close about her, but she was silent, inwardly frightened and disturbed at the dénouement to the dinner. But Jacobelli was elated and highly amused. He occupied the uptown seat himself, and sat with a hand resting on each knee, complacent and benignant.

"Cara mia, I salute!" he exclaimed happily. "You are an actress as well as a singer. You could not possibly have entertained him better or interested him more piquantly."

"I did not try to interest him," Carlota replied, wearily. "I hate him and the look in his eyes."

She drew in her breath sharply with a tremor of dread, and returned the quick, understanding pressure of Maria's hand. But the maestro merely smiled at them both, smiled until his round, plump face seemed like a caricature of himself sketched in upturned half-moons of mirth.

"That is quite all right," he assured her. "You should be proud that so great a man is attracted by your genius. So soon as you have signed your first contract, my dear, and made your début, then you may refuse to see him, if you like, if not before. What is the look in his eyes to you? Thousands will gaze at you so. You must learn to accept homage gracefully. Ward is a stepping-stone to success. To-morrow I shall see Casanova for you as he ordered."

Carlota closed her eyes as the car drew up under the heavy porte-cochère at the Saint Germain apartments. Its rim of electric lights was the sole illumination on the dark side street at that hour.

"No, I shall not come up with you," protested Jacobelli. "Do not tempt me, signora. I shall overeat if you set before me one of those delightful suppers of yours, and, besides, the child must rest. We may get a hearing tomorrow and she needs all her strength. Sleep well, Carlota. Remember, smother the emotion that cripples your work."

She did not speak until they reached their apartment, and Maria laid her hands on her shoulders to look closely into her eyes under the shaded lights.

"Ah, my dear one, they have hurt you tonight," she sighed. "You are not ready yet, not old enough to manage these men. Some day it will be as nothing to you, their whims and notions, their mad passions and threats. A man in love is the most helpless, pitiful thing in all the world, never, never dangerous. You have him at your mercy. What did he say to you?"

Carlota slipped out of her velvet cloak tiredly.

"I hardly know. It was so sudden and horrible, the touch of his hands on my flesh, and his face close to mine. He was a dog to take advantage of my being there as his guest—"

"Oh, hush! What did he say to you?" urged Maria shrewdly.

"Nothing at all. He asked me to sing, and when I had finished he seized me in his arms and tried to kiss me."

"I should not have left you alone. Opportunity makes the thief. It is Jacobelli's fault. He must have known that Ward desired a chance of speaking to you. But it is all nothing, cara mia, nothing at all. It was certain he would fall in love with you. No man could help it, but he must be taught some gems are priceless. He did not ask you any questions, then, about yourself, about the Paoli collection or the jewels you wore?"

Carlota looked at her wonderingly.

"Of course not. Why should he?"

"I do not want any one to know they are here in America, out of the Tittani vaults. Nobody is aware of it as yet excepting yourself and the Marchese. He helped me with the customs when we came in, he and the delightful Palmieri. But even to Palmieri they were merely jewels. He did not know their histories."

Carlota watched her anxiously, a quick reaction of tenderness and solicitude for Maria sweeping over her, and making her forgetful of her own trouble.

"You're worried, dear. Why?" she asked.

"Why?" Maria laughed. "Because I am doubtless a superstitious old fool. Paoli always said there was a curse about the rubies and pearls, rubies for the blood of the people, pearls for the tears they shed. I wish we had not brought them."

CHAPTER IX

The following morning at nine-thirty, Signor Jacobelli stood bowing on the threshold of Casanova's small sanctum in the Opera building. Armed with Ogden Ward's influence and his own reputation, his welcome was assured. Casanova, lean and dark, beamed on his visitor like some comradely Mephisto luxuriating in dolce far niente.

"Come in, my friend," he called. "You release me from the duty of perusing the new opera of the great, unknown composer who insists that I shall discover him. Do you bring me a new sensation?"

But Jacobelli was mysterious and secretive. For over an hour he sat in the famous, three-cornered office, dilating upon the beauty and genius of Paoli's granddaughter until he knew he held the interest of the impresario. Suddenly Alphonse, the slender, solicitous secretary, peered around the door.

"Mrs. Carrington Nevins," he whispered tentatively. "She is alone."

"You will wait," Casanova urged, as he nodded assent. "She is very wealthy, one of our best subscribers. She wishes to secure some good singers for her Italian fête. One cannot refuse, and then she has a daughter whom she thinks is a Galli-Curci handicapped by position and money."

"I fly," answered Jacobelli shortly, but as he turned about, he encountered Mrs. Nevins. Somehow, with her elaborately arranged gray hair, fine aquiline profile, and costume of gray velvet trimmed in silver fox, she brought a memory of Marie Antoinette, or was it merely the reminder of some famous actress in the part? The old maestro paused before her, a half-comic air of having been captured on the point of flight.

"I have heard often of you," she said graciously. "My daughter Nathalie sings. She is a wonderful child, and even you, signor, must recognize genius, though you meet it handicapped."

Casanova's half-closed eyes twinkled at the inference, but Jacobelli was in a mellow mood.

"I shall be charmed to hear her some time, madame. Let her not choke her voice upon her golden spoon."

"You must hear her soon," insisted Mrs. Nevins. "I am getting up a programme for my Italian fête, the milk fund for the children, you know, a wonderful cause. Don't you think Signor Jacobelli might be a help to us, Signor Casanova? I do want to have everything in harmony, authentic and still startling. I want a little operetta for Nathalie's sake, and have been talking over the libretto with a young composer I just met, Griffeth Ames; perhaps you may know him."

But Jacobelli was in a hurry to leave, and protesting his utter ignorance of Mr. Ames's existence, he departed, not realizing how the grim sisters of fate had tangled his thread of life that moment with Griffeth Ames's destiny.

At the same moment Ames sat perched on the seat in the slanting dormer window, staring down moodily at the street below. It was nearly eleven. Sometimes she came in the morning, and they would have lunch together after her lesson. He had not realized how deep an interest she had become in his life until two days had elapsed without her. Ptolemy kept vigil with him through the long evenings, while he smoked and told himself all sophists and philosophers were bachelors and liars. Love was a terrible, disconcerting truth. And he saw Carlota's face in the vanishing rings of his smoke.

At the corner stood a pushcart piled high with California grapes, turned into a shrine of Bacchus. Upreared on a wooden framework festoons of clusters dangled temptingly, and vine leaves were twined about the base of the cart. The boy who tended it bartered with an old sibyl-faced Sicilian grandmother, naming her a price, and whistling until she came around to it. And suddenly Ames caught sight of Carlota as she walked across the Square from the 'bus terminus, her slim, youthful figure conspicuous among the vari-clad denizens of the park. She paused at the stand and bought plentifully, not only of the grapes, but of late rich-toned pears and golden-russet apples. He leaned far out the window, watching her longingly, Ptolemy rubbing against his arm as though he, too, sensed the return of Columbine.

At the foot of the last flight of stairs Carlota hesitated, listening. From the studio came a new melody, a haunting, yearning strain that she remembered. Ames had played it at the Phelpses that first night when their eyes had met. He had named it the *Quest of Love, Cerca di Amore*. As it ended, she opened the door softly, without knocking.

"I have come to prepare lunch, signor," she said demurely, but with a flash of mischief in her eyes. "If you are still angry, then Ptolemy and I will eat it together."

"Is it a lasting peace or merely an armistice?" he demanded, sweeping the papers from the table. "You are afraid to look at me for fear you will surrender."

"It is an armistice," she said sedately. "It is beneath your dignity as a composer to take pupils who have not real genius. I still hold to that. And I shall need celery and romaine and tomatoes and grapefruit and almonds for my salad, so you may go out and find them."

She tied a strip of drapery around her for an apron, and started preparations for lunch. Ames leaned from a back window and hailed a small and willing neighbor to go to the market, after the needs of the queen, as he said.

They did not speak to each other for some time. Ames watched her as the sunlight poured down on her bowed head. He held a melon in one hand, uplifted absently, a length of scarlet and black art burlap around his waist.

"You look exactly like one of the melon-sellers on the quay at Naples," she told him, with a little smile. "When the boat stops there, they crowd around begging you to buy from them. Lift up your arm and call out."

"I will do no such thing," responded Ames buoyantly. "I decline to pose for your majesty. Will you deign to name your castle habitat, that I may call on your most royal parents and interest them in my humble self?"

She was serious in an instant.

"I have no people, signor. If you could go with me to the Villa Tittani, you would find a very little village high up on the rocks above the Campagna. You know where I mean? See?"

She dipped her finger-tips in the dregs of chianti remaining in the bowl beside her where she had used it in the salad dressing, and traced a map for him on the bare table-top.

"Here is the winding road from the shore, and here at the very top there is a villa with rose-tinted stone walls all about it, very high walls overgrown with flowers and vines. That is where the nobility live." Her eyes were sparkling with mischief. "Often when I was little I have seen the Contessa walking on the terraces. She was so stately and handsome, and her daughter Bianca was like a real princess should be, a princess of dreams and fairy-tales, tall and slender and with eyes like stars. Then, if you walk on, down through the ilex avenue, you will come to a very quiet spot where the old tombs face the sea, and there are my people, all of them."

"I'm a brute!" exclaimed Ames, holding her hands in his with quick, understanding tenderness. "The way I have let you come and go without showing any real interest after all you have done for me."

"What have I done? Come down here and let you teach me and in return told you some fairy-tales."

He stared down at her, puzzled as always. He was twenty-four, and the coasts of chance and illusion were far more tangible to him than any of Life's ports of call. He wondered if he could make her understand all that she had become to him. He wheeled about and found his pipe with sudden disgust at his own impotence.

"Carlota, do you know, I've just discovered something about myself. I'm a beastly poor amateur at making love. I want to tell you just how I feel about you slipping in here like a sunbeam, or—or Ptolemy. You know, I found him on the fire escape one morning, and he's stayed here ever since. There was a sparrow, too, last winter. I left my window open there, and it flew in out of the storm and perched on the curtain rod. Fought me every time I tried to feed it. You seemed to belong to their crowd, the sunbeam and the sparrow and Ptolemy. You just came and stayed, and I was a fool; I took you for granted."

"You asked me to come, after we first met," Carlota corrected him. "I would not come without the invitation first."

He bowed low before her.

"And I am honored by the royal presence. I have learned these last two days the strangest thing. When you are here and we are friends, I can work at my best, and when you are angry with me, it goes just like that, all my inspiration. So you see you have me at your mercy." He turned and rummaged among the mass of papers and score-sheets on the piano-top. "I'm going to finish my operetta in a week if you'll stand by me and not get temperamental, dear. The big chance is coming now. Mrs. Nevins says she can get me an immediate hearing from Casanova if she presents it first at her fête. Isn't that great?"

Carlota's lips pressed together firmly at the name. She did not answer.

"You must be glad with me because you gave me the idea for it. I had been tormented with a mass of harmonies and tunes that would not shape into anything. Remember how I played that first night you met me? Listen to this and see if you remember it."

He leaned over the piano towards her, reading aloud the synopsis of the libretto.

"Fiametta is the lonely princess of the Castle Tittani. She loves Peppino, a fisher-boy. There is a fête in the village. She disguises herself to go down and mingle with the people, scaling the walls of Tittani with love's magic. She dances with Peppino, who does not know that she is the princess. He is disguised as Harlequin. His sweetheart stabs her through jealousy when Peppino avows his love for her. She dies in his arms as the people recognize her as their princess. It is the tragedy of youth's eternal quest for love beyond all barriers."

Her head was bent over the salad bowl as she listened.

"I call it *Fiametta*. Do you like it?" he asked eagerly. "You don't mind my using the little story you told me, do you, Carlota? I may make it immortal."

"Why must she die, your princess?" she said wistfully. "I love it all but that. How could you write it when you had not seen our beautiful Tittani or known my people."

"I had seen and known you. That's the answer. Listen to this." He flung himself down at the piano, head back, striking into the melody that had been his call to her. "This is your motif."

Suddenly there came an imperative tap at the door.

"Open. My arms are full."

"That's only Dmitri. You met him at the Phelpses that night." Ames threw wide the door. "Enter and join the happy throng. Comes a Greek bearing gifts."

At sight of Carlota, Dmitri dropped his bundles and made obeisance with sedate ceremony.

"I had not dreamt that any but myself would ever climb those stairs to the house of Ptolemy."

"I'm the luckiest man in the world. Listen, Dmitri; quit bowing and understand. This is—" Ames hesitated and laughed. "I don't even know your last name, Carlota. You tell him. You met each other at Phelps's."

Carlota looked at the newcomer in her grave, measuring way. She had not remembered him at all. He was older than Ames, and without any claims whatever to good looks. Swarthy, thin, slight, stoop-shouldered, careless in dress, there was still something indefinably distinguished and reassuring about him. He might have sat for a bust of the youthful Socrates with his blunt, uneven profile. A perpetual smile perched on his wide mouth; not a propitiatory smile, but rather a tolerant one. Here was a spirit that might have waited æons on the edge of chaos, believing absolutely in the ultimate birth of cosmic harmony, even on earth.

"Please! I beg you not to." He interrupted her. "I do not wish to know your name. Identity is the cloak of selfishness. They number convicts and name hapless infants. Human consciousness is a universal lottery where the lucky numbers win by drawing personality in lots of genius. Griffeth is a genius. I am one. You, too, with that face, do not have to be a genius. You are Woman, incarnate Love and Inspiration to us poor devils."

"Give him work to keep him quiet," advised Ames.

But Dmitri picked up his bundles and began opening them with the air of a high priest at his ritual.

"I shall prepare a feast for you today, a treat. The brigand stew of Bulgaria. I have eaten it on mountain heights where even the goats die of starvation."

"I think I will go," Carlota said in her quick, aloof way, and Dmitri turned to her eagerly, his face full of a strange, beseeching charm.

"See, I have disappointed you!" he declared; "when for weeks I have hoped to catch you here on one of your flights of passage. First when I saw you at Mr. Phelps's, you overlooked me absolutely for him." He nodded at Ames. "He is merely spectacular. He had no more vision, no wider horizons than a mole. When he told me yesterday that you would never come here again, I understood perfectly. I told him you would surely return, but I knew also why you were angry with him. He stands outside our range of perspective, so you must forgive him. He blunders like a baby lamb; you know the kind with large knees and prodigious ears, utterly hopeless."

"Grand old Diogenes; all he needs is a tub and lantern to go into business." Ames patted him affectionately. "Put your old lamb on to stew and stop spouting if we are to eat it today. What do you do first, braise it?"

"Let it alone. He is become the plaything of the privileged classes." Dmitri seized his bundles and made for the kitchenette, where he declaimed just the same. "How many times in three days have you motored down to Long Island? Confess."

Ames avoided Carlota's questioning, accusing eyes.

"Twice, to give lessons."

"Twice for lessons, and then you stay all the afternoon and have dinner also there. The truth ye cannot bear."

"When I believed that you were working hard on your opera and were sorry I did not come back to you," Carlota said softly.

"Son of discordance!" Ames flung a cushion headlong over the partition. "You only want to set Carlota against me and seize her yourself."

"See?" Dmitri's head showed around the curtain delightedly. "He has already the little social tricks. To be petty. Still, I like him, so I will save him. You shall not become the Harlequin boy of the nouveaux riches. They will but monopolize your time until a new warrior of ennui shall appear and grasp the golden bough from your hand. They will permit you to loll in their beautiful playgrounds until you imagine yourself indispensable. You will think you are succeeding, getting in on the inside, as they say. You will gain patronage. You are young and might be popular, but time is your treasure, and they waste it as nothing."

Out of doors spring dallied in the old square, and Jacobelli, stepping from the interior of a green motor 'bus just beyond the Arch, lingered to regard almost paternally the toddling, black-eyed babies and fluttering, dancing youngsters that played around the dry fountain. A flock of pigeons swerved down from the Judson Memorial Tower and he smiled at them benignly, seeing those that fed at noon below the Campanile.

He had tried to induce Casanova to join him at luncheon down at the Brevoort, but the director had another engagement and Jacobelli had been forced to come alone, something he innately disliked. There was the genial, gregarious instinct of the old Roman feaster in the maestro. He loved to treat himself to a carefully chosen meal in a favorite corner, with a friend opposite, and a chef on duty who knew his name.

The beauty of the Square lured him. In late October it seemed to rest like some gypsy dancer, garbed in rich attire of red and gold, but silent and tense with expectation of the next twirl. He strolled towards the south side leisurely, intending to circle the Square on his way back to the hotel, trying to reason with himself on his duty to Carlota. His experience with women had taught him the usual causes of their temperamental moods. Something had undoubtedly aroused Carlota's nature into sudden and unexpected sensitiveness. It could not be merely her dislike and resentment towards Ward. If this had been so, then why had she not reacted under the stimulus during the past two years. No, he mused, with toleration, somehow, the contagion of Love had touched her in spite of their care, and lo, the walls of Tittani tumbled at the magic bugle of some Childe Roland. Even so, it was nothing serious, he told himself. Maria's health was better now. She could watch her closer. At eighteen a girl's imagination will clothe some distant object with all the splendor of heroism. Doubtless she was under the spell of her own natural yearning for love.

And suddenly, even while he rambled and reasoned, the demigod of Misrule wakened drowsily and took note of the excellent juxtaposition of certain humans. Jacobelli stopped dead short, head uplifted like a horse scenting fire as a voice floated out on the midday air singing Mimi's duet with a lilting, impetuous tenor for company. He could have sworn it was Carlota. Never could there be two such voices in New York. He tried to locate the sound, but it seemed to float from him elusively. He cut hastily across the southwest end of the park, seeking it, and gazed up at the row of brownstone old studio buildings across Fourth Street.

At the same moment a young Bulgarian, smoking a thin long cigarette in the exact center of his lips, rose from a seat and followed him. When Jacobelli crossed the street, intent and purpose in every move of his rotund figure, the boy waited, his seal-brown eyes mere slits, half-lifted lids showing gleams of high lights as he stared fixedly after him. Outside the narrow flagged plots, the old teacher hesitated, then entered the dusty hallway of the house next to Ames's abiding-place. The Bulgarian smiled and followed after him, lingering at the corner.

Up in the studio luncheon was over. So successful and opulent it had been, this brigand feast, that Dmitri announced they were all suffering from the ennui of satiety, that bête noire of the rich. Carlota was happy once more. She had read over the libretto of the operetta while the two argued over points in the score, had sat at the piano, trying bits here and there of Fiametta's rôle until, somewhere down on Bleecker Street, a church chime reached her ears, and she rose hurriedly. Maria would be home at two.

"I must leave you," she said regretfully. "And all the dishes to wash!"

"I'll do them gladly." Dmitri donned an apron promptly. "Griff, you take your inspiration to the 'bus while I do your work for you."

"How do you know that I take the 'bus to my home?"

She looked back at him teasingly. He waved both hands comprehensively, dismissing the query as superfluous.

"Everybody who comes down here takes the 'bus. It is part of the thrill, the experience of the unusual. They are the land ferries that cross the gulf between fact and fancy."

He began the duet plaintively as he fished for a strip of drapery and tossed it about his shoulders for a cloak. Carlota took up the reply of Mimi while she pulled a black-velvet student cap over her close, glossy ripples of hair. Out on the landing Ames waited for her eagerly.

"Listen. You will come again soon, won't you, dear? Dmitri's a curious sort, but he's all gold, no alloy. He thinks your voice is great."

"I like him very much," she said naïvely. "Much better than Mrs. Nevins and her daughter. How many times must you go to see them this week?"

"Oh, don't! It isn't anything at all, her interest in my work. She's giving some sort of a fête for the Italian Relief Fund, a sort of glorified musicale as I understand it, and she wants me to give my operetta so her daughter can sing the mezzo part, Pippa. I intend that you shall sing Fiametta, the princess."

"Impossible!" exclaimed Carlota in hushed alarm. "I never, never could do that, Mr. Ames."

"You call me Griffeth," he swung back happily. "You are going to sing it just the same, and it may make your fortune. I know it will mine. Dmitri's all wrong, you know. He's got some sort of a brain kink over this hatred of the rich. I don't dare tell him even who my father is for fear he may cut my acquaintance."

"Is your father, then, rich?" Her gaze never left his face.

"Well, they call him so where we live out in Colorado. You're in the bondholder class there after you pass fifty thousand, but I don't think Dad's in danger of being counted an enemy of the people yet; just comfortably dusted."

He laughed down at her as they crossed the Square towards the 'bus terminus. And at exactly the same instant Signor Jacobelli was bursting without warning or ceremony into a studio on the second floor where a model posed. He emerged, nonplussed and furious. On the third floor the door was locked. He shook the handle imperatively, and a disturbed but pleasantly modulated voice answered:

"Sorry, old man. Come Monday, will you?"

"It is impossible," exclaimed the maestro to himself, when he reached the street, and stood wiping his forehead with a sense of baffled uncertainty. "Yet there are not two voices like hers in the world. I shall not wait. Love is a madness."

He retraced his steps towards the Brevoort, determined now to tell Maria his suspicions. Up at the dormer window of the studio, Dmitri leaned out, placing bread crumbs on the fire escape for the sparrows.

"Go to, greedy one," he said gravely, to one brown vagrant struggling after the largest piece. "You elbow for room in the bread-line. Beware the Infinite overlooks your falling."

He glanced at the picture ensemble of the Square, one eye half closed to catch the light-and-shade effect and found a hindrance suddenly to his enjoyment of life. Sauntering across the street and into the park entrance was the Bulgarian. He paused to drink at the little iron fountain, and Dmitri leaned forward, giving a low, peculiar whistle. The boy lifted his head with a jerk and stared about him. He forgot his thirst. The crafty, self-contained air fell from him. Dmitri laughed down at him and waved his hand, beckoning him to come up. The other shook his head and waited.

"Another sparrow," Dmitri said to himself as he closed the studio and went to join him. "He is too thin, much too thin."

CHAPTER X

When Ames returned to the studio twenty minutes later, it was still empty. In his own room over on East Twenty-Eighth Street, Dmitri sat on a couch, smoking and listening to the boy Steccho talk of Sofia, of his mountain home, of Maryna his sister, and the little smiling mother who cooked so excellently.

"The last time we met, we dipped in the same drinking-bowl, remember?" Dmitri smiled across at him. "You are too young to come here in these times. Who has sent you? Do not tell me if you dare not. I am not afraid. I will still open wide the door every time you care to visit me, my friend. Are the little mother and sister quite safe, you are sure?"

"Oh, absolutely." Steccho's dark face glowed with enthusiasm. "Before I come here I see to that, and they will have more still, much more."

"So? Then you are doing well. That is good. The times are changing about, eh? Are there any of the others here? I have met no one since I came. I was wounded and in the hospital for months, so I have lost track of the old friends."

"You did not return, then, afterwards?" Steccho's glance was uneasy.

"No," replied Dmitri, lying on his back, and blowing long, uneven ovals into the air. "I do not like it all, frankly, my boy. They compromise and barter first with this faction, then with the other. Each is afraid to trust the other. It has become a great struggle for self-preservation now that the masters twist the torture screws of starvation. Life, after all, once you desert nature, becomes merely a struggle for the dear old bread and butter in one form or another. Commerce is built upon the necessities of human existence under modern conditions. Personally, I am very radical on one point. I would kill without mercy the man who gambles for his own profit on the necessities of his brother man, his food, his fuel, his clothing.

And I do not believe in killing, as you know. I regard war as a subterfuge, an exploitation of power. I object to persons infusing into my mind hatred of my brother man merely because he happens to live on a different spot of earth than I do, and belongs to a different branch of the same human race."

"There are robbers and murderers in the brotherhood as well as in the privileged classes."

"So, my Steccho has learned to perch safely and sensibly upon the fence between the warring factions, yes? The rain falls on the just and the unjust, therefore we must be merciful likewise." He sat up and reached for his violin, playing stray chords, bits of folk-songs and haunting Czech melodies in minors.

Steccho listened moodily, his eyes almost closed as he clasped arms about his knees, and bent his head on them. Dmitri played in silence for nearly half an hour. When he stopped, the boy looked up at him wistfully.

"When the cause is right, the way must be right too."

"What do you mean by the cause?" Dmitri asked genially. "We live in a day when causes are hung for sale in any market-place. You may buy them like indulgences from pilgrim friars. I would pick my cause with caution."

"I mean this. No matter what we do, if it is for some great, beautiful purpose, then it does not matter, eh?"

"You will stub your toe on that rock, the end that justifies the means; that is all it comes to when you are through with reasoning and sophistry. And I do not like any reasoning which may be diverted by the idiot Chance, to his own blind folly. Can you tell me frankly why you are here? I will keep silent and help you if I may."

Steccho threw away his last cigarette and rose, stretching himself like an animal impatient for a run.

"I am here so that my mother and Maryna may dwell in the yellow castle forever," he answered with a slow smile. "You cannot help, but I should like to come here and rest now and then."

"You will come again soon, my friend," Dmitri laid both hands on his shoulders warmly. "Come often, when you like. If I am out, look for me over in the squares, or open the door and be happy as you can until I return. Light the fire yourself. It awaits you. If you will come back tonight, I can promise you such a meal of broiled lamb and rice as you have not tasted since the home days."

"Not tonight." Steccho shook his head. "I might take you from your friends. I could hear you singing while I stood in the park there today. The girl had a fine voice."

"She has genius and is poor. My friend is giving her lessons so she may sing in his opera some day. He is very much interested in her. It is a romance." Dmitri smiled whimsically. "He does not even know her name, but she is very beautiful. Ah, my Steccho, if you and I, who are older than the ages in our outlook on life, could only receive this baptism of joy, this love. You would forget your torches and rivers of blood if the one woman would give you her lips, yes?"

The boy turned his back on him at the door, the face of Carlota before his eyes as it had disturbed and bewildered his purpose ever since he had first looked upon its beauty and innocence. His fingers shook as he fumbled blindly for the doorknob.

"I will come again, Dmitri. Good-night."

He went directly uptown in the subway. There is a small carriage entrance to the Hotel Dupont. By it, you may enter most privately and unostentatiously a low-ceiled, satin-walled corridor which leads past a flower-stand and telephone booth to a single elevator, half concealed in a recess.

Here the boy waited while his name was sent up to Count Lazio Jurka. There was a delay, and presently down in the private elevator came the valet and personal courier of the Count, a soldierly individual, gray-haired and austere.

"You always blunder," he said as he led the way to the servants' elevator. "You come here as a tailor, not a guest. He does not expect you tonight. Have you news?"

Steccho shrugged his shoulders sullenly. After the meeting with Dmitri his mind was unsettled. As they passed by the palm-guarded tea-room, the great paneled dining-room on the corner, the rotunda with its rose-hued walls and marble columns, the leisurely parade of the late afternoon frequenters, his memory traveled rapidly back to his old life that Dmitri had been a part of.

It was a far cry to Rigl, his home village, eighteen miles out of Sofia if you take the narrow mountain trail on horseback. There had been the childhood there, and later, when he had worked in Sofia at the little hand-press bindery, to enable himself to study evenings. He passed one hand over his eyes restlessly as the valet opened the door of a corner suite on the eighth floor and snapped the catch after them. The small inner salon was empty. Excepting for scattered daily papers it bore no trace of use. The door of the dressing-room was ajar, and Steccho bowed low on its threshold, waiting the word to enter.

Before a large oval mirror Count Jurka tied his cravat with a deliberate and distinct enjoyment of the artistry required by the operation. Clad in underclothes and shirt, he resembled some French courtier, one who might have just flung off his cloak and hat in a gray dawn rendezvous, and, balancing his rapier, awaited his opponent.

He was youthful, blond, serene-eyed, the Count Jurka. Throughout the war of nations those same blue eyes had witnessed unspeakable atrocities with the utmost impersonal calm. The white, pink-nailed hands that dallied over cravats had dipped in the blood of innocents quite as artistically and deliberately as they handled the silk ends now. He was an individual the guillotine would have licked its long steel tongue over after devouring, but there were no guillotines in Sofia, and firing-squads were out of date likewise. The hand of fate deputed its blows to those who worked secretly and left no trace behind save the victim.

"Come in, Steccho," he called pleasantly. "How goes this merry world with you? The cigarettes, Georges."

Steccho accepted two from the long, narrow brown leather box the valet extended to him, and held them unlighted in his fingers. There had been a man in Sofia who had been extremely ill, even to the verge of death, after smoking cigarettes from that brown leather box.

The cravat tied, Jurka seated himself in an amber satin armchair, a black-velvet dressing-robe about his shoulders. He smiled musingly across at the boy, noting his drawn, harassed face. The hand that held the cigarettes shook slightly. The muscles around his lips twitched under that amused scrutiny.

"Have you found them?"

The question came hard and short finally. Steccho shook his head.

"Excellenza," he said eagerly, "the opportunity has not come. I have followed them both unceasingly, day and night, and have seen nothing."

"You have followed the girl. Day and night you have followed her, no one else. You have not yet ascertained where the jewels are kept, nor whether she has access to them. Are they in New York or in Italy? Are they in the possession of Maria Roma in their apartment, or in a safety-deposit vault? Why do you shadow the girl Carlota unless you are perhaps in love with her?"

Steccho's eyes were brilliant with resentment that he dared not express in words.

"One must go slowly here, excellenza," he said. "It is not Sofia. You yourself would not have the power to shield me or hold the jewels if I were caught. One must look the ground over thoroughly. Possibly, as you say, they are not even here in America, but have been left in Italy."

Jurka smiled slowly.

"I will satisfy you on that point, and relieve your doubt, my Steccho. They are here. Duty was declared on the full collection, Palmieri tells me. It passed as the private jewels of a non-resident alien. So far, I do not believe Ogden Ward has even seen them, but I know the girl has offered them to him in return for the sums he has advanced for her musical education. She has no conception of their value."

"You know she has offered them to him, excellenza!" Steccho's head was thrust forward eagerly, the emphasis in his tone conveying his incredulity.

"Through Ward's Japanese butler, Ishigaki. He overheard her the night Ward gave the girl a dinner."

"Excellenza, your eyes are everywhere," murmured the boy.

"Not my eyes, Steccho," smiled Jurka. "My gold. Georges here is an able and cautious distributor, eh? Does the girl Carlota never wear her jewels?"

He stretched out his feet carelessly for Georges to fasten his boots. The boy watched him with unblinking eyes, thinking of how once he had seen their high, hard heels grind into the dead face of a man lying in the snow. He was the friend of Dmitri and his group then. The war had seemed far from their little mountain village until there came a day when Jurka's troops came through. They had quartered at the inn and scattered among the different homes. Levano, old Levano, who preached liberty and peace from his blacksmith forge, had staggered out into the road after his two daughters had been violated, and had thrust his red-hot branding-irons into the face of the soldiery. Jurka had ground his heel on his mouth that had stiffened under choked curses.

Later, in an upper room at the inn—He stared fixedly at the highly polished boots of Jurka, and sought to fasten his memory solely on Maryna and the little mother. The Count had said Maryna was a pretty little thing the day he had saved Steccho from the troops. She had run through the crowd in the village and had knelt to wipe her brother's bruised face. That was the first time he had seen her, and she was barely fifteen. It had been later on, in the upper room at the inn, that Steccho had sworn to enter the service of the Queen providing safety might be assured the two left at Rigl. Whenever, as now, he was tempted to spring at the white, self-assured throat, he forced himself to think of them. He had come tonight primarily to ask if they were still safe, if his excellenza had any news from Rigl, and to shake off the disquieting effect of Dmitri's philosophy.

"I have never seen her wear jewels, excellenza," he answered slowly. "She is very young, about sixteen. They would not permit it, probably."

"She is nineteen and looks older," returned the Count curtly.

"Pardon—you have then seen her?"

Jurka made no reply, but met the boy's eager gaze with calculating suspicion.

"You are feeling your way through the dark, Steccho. Beware of pricking swords. You have been allotted a certain task, a very easy task, merely to find out where these jewels are if they are concealed in the apartment of Carlota Trelango, and to get them at all risks. You have two women as opponents, and you crawl and creep and shadow them for weeks. You were told to enter their abode and search it. You were told to find out their associates, their circumstances. What have you accomplished save the incessant following of the girl herself. Are you then infatuated, my Steccho? It is the eternal failing of youth."

Steccho's face colored dully. Maryna was fifteen, the girl Carlota only four years older. Most of the young girls of Rigl had been given to the Jurka's soldiery that week, excepting the three loveliest—little Roziska, the pale Wanda destined for the convent, and radiant Katinka with eyes like Carlota's, velvety, luminous. He had always watched her in church when she knelt in the long shaft of purple light above the aureole of Saint Genevieve. If there had been no war, he would have married Katinka some day, but the three had been dragged to the rooms above the inn, reserved for the high honor of his excellenza's favor. Were the jewels but part of his plan? If he had seen Carlota's beauty, would she not become like the three girls he had seen thrown out to the soldiers after his excellenza had wearied of them? He lifted keen eyes to the suave, smiling face.

"They go nowhere, save to the places I have already told you."

Georges grimaced at his servility and protesting palms.

"Recount!" ordered Jurka. "The Marchese, Ward, Jacobelli. Are there more?"

"No more." The boy's gaze never wavered. Dmitri had said it was a romance, the affair in the Square, and they were his friends. It gave him a curious, inmost thrill of happiness to feel that he was thwarting the man who had killed the other girl, Katinka.

The bell of the suite rang lightly. Georges sprang to his feet, laying an evening suit over the boy's arm, and pushing him before him into the reception-hall. As he opened the door, he gave voluble directions to the tailor's assistant for the evening garb of the Count. The hotel page presented several letters on a silver tray and passed on down the corridor.

"It is not safe for you to come here." Jurka opened the letters with a single thrust of a slender blade. His clean-cut dexterity fascinated Steccho. "Where the devil do you live, anyway?"

"Twenty-Eighth Street, East," he lied simply. "I change often. A friend told me of this place."

"Make no friends, I have told you."

"A former friend whom I had known in Sofia. I but met him on the street one day, a very old man, Boris—"

Georges held up his hand with a frown. The Count perused the first letter he opened twice, and smiled. It was from Mrs. Carrington Nevins, urgently requesting his presence and assistance in the success of her entertainment at Belvoir, Long Island.

"The social ruse always wins out, Georges. We are the emissaries of the queen's mercy; we wish to study the methods for rehabilitating the wounded, for salvaging the war wreckage of humanity. The exiled queen's heart is torn with remorse for her poor lost ones. It sounds well and opens many doors, among them, Belvoir." He laughed and tossed the letter to Georges. "Accept. It is for a week from Saturday."

Steccho waited his pleasure by the door. Timidly, as Jurka went through his mail, he ventured to attract his attention once more.

"Excellenza, you have heard some news recently, perhaps from Sofia, from Rigl?"

Georges motioned him to leave, but he lingered obstinately.

"You have news of my mother and sister, yes, of Maryna, excellenza? You remember Maryna, the little girl who—"

The Count nodded his blond head towards the door.

"Out!" he said briefly. "Bring me the jewels by Saturday."

CHAPTER XI

Signor Jacobelli was in a baffled mood. Every time Carlota came for her lesson, he would regard her thoughtfully, dubiously, but found no solution to his problem in her happy, serene face and dark eyes that held a gleam of mirth nowadays.

Once she had just missed meeting Ward himself there. It had been his first visit since the dinner, and after his departure a florist's messenger brought her a purple box filled with single-petaled Parma violets. Under them lay a velvet case containing a pendant, two perfect, pear-shaped pearls. She retained the messenger, writing on the back of Ward's own card in haste:

> Signor: I thank you. The only jewels I ever wear are those of my grandmother!
>
> Carlota Trelango.

"And the flowers—behold!" she flung up a window and leaned far out to throw them down into the street. A street piano played below, the wife of the owner turning the crank with a stout bambino on one hip. "You throw her some money now, maestro, so that both soul and body are fed. Who was it said, bread for the body, white hyacinths—" She checked herself, recalling suddenly that it had been Dmitri who loved to chant Mahomet's axiom, but Jacobelli had not even noticed it. Grumblingly he dropped a crumpled bill to the woman's extended apron.

"You are not a spoiled child any longer," he told Carlota. "You are now a person of destiny. Why, then, do you persist in acting like a petulant marionette instead of the dignified artiste. You cannot afford to rebuff Ward. He is your patron. You are merely a little beggar on the doorstep of hope, my child, and you take on the airs of a queen."

"And here you have been telling me all along that I must learn to be queenlike and aloof." Carlota sat back in the winged armchair beside the fireplace. It was far too deep and too high for her, having been selected solely to accommodate the rotund proportions of Jacobelli, but she preferred it. Some way, it had the significance of a throne chair when she felt herself holding the balance of power, as now. "And if I am a person of destiny, then how can anything that I do alter events?" She laughed up at him softly, teasingly. He looked away from her in somber disapproval. "Oh, my dear, dear good teacher and friend," she pleaded with swift reaction. "Forgive me. I will try, indeed I will. What do you want me to do? Anything but see Mr. Ward alone."

"You shall prepare for your début." Jacobelli took up her challenge instantly. "Casanova will place you on the list for next season. That will give you an entire year for more study. And you shall flame forth in glory as Margherita or Gilda—"

"Why not Santuzza or Aïda?" Carlota's temper rose at his suggestion. "Let me sing these, my maestro, when I am stout and placid some day, but now, give me the new rôles."

"You seek the spectacular," he accused. "You would be like all of the women. They must have the greatest rôle of all written for them alone, dedicated to them. Ah, do I not know!"

Maria arrived in time to prevent his tirade against whims. She listened in delight as he told of the interview with Casanova.

"After it is all settled, she will be sweet and docile once more," she promised. "She has not been the same even to me since that night at Mr. Ward's."

"You think that is the reason, eh?" Jacobelli stared moodily before him, feeling it was the proper time to enlighten Maria. And yet, how? Were not his suspicions based on air? Only the voice down in the Square was actually proof to himself, and how could he prove it to others, when he had not even traced it?

"For one thing, she is studying too hard, I think," Maria pursued earnestly. "Four lessons a week and such long ones; are they not too much for the child, signor?"

"Four?" repeated Jacobelli, one bushy eyebrow lifting in amazement. "She tells you she has four lessons a week?"

"Two hours in the morning, two in the afternoon. It is very strenuous, I think."

"Doubtless so." He rose and paced the floor with rising agitation. Carlota had come to his studio three times each week, for a two-hour lesson only. Here was proof positive that she was straying somewhere into forbidden paths. "It is absolutely imperative, signora," he began huskily, when the suspected one came from the inner room, humming to herself from the love tragedy of Mélisande. "Imperative that she make her début next year," he finished conclusively. "Delays are dangerous, especially when one is overstudying."

The hidden rebuke passed completely by Carlota, as she said good-bye, sparkling and confident, and Jacobelli pondered, with a sense of responsibility, feeling that he alone knew the real reason for her deception. Possibly Ptolemy or Dmitri might have enlightened him still further. Necessarily Carlota's visits had become more frequent, since she was to sing the leading rôle in Ames's operetta. He had won her consent after many arguments and stormy scenes. Six times in one week he had been summoned to Belvoir to consult with Mrs. Nevins about her fête. Four times the black car with its buff and old gold interior had waited his convenience outside the old brownstone row on Fourth Street, and when Carlota arrived for her lesson, she had found only Ptolemy in possession. Yet Ames had argued her into agreeing with him, that this was his great opportunity to present his operetta under the most favorable auspices.

"And you are to sing Fiametta," he told her positively. "You are the perfect type for her, dear, a slim, aloof little princess, questing for love. Can you get the two costumes, the peasant's for the fête, and the princess's when she is in the castle? I suppose you could manage the first out of your own wardrobe, and we will have to rent the other royal raiment."

He was like a boy over the fun of actually preparing the production. Carlota looked at him unforgivingly, even appraisingly, if one could appraise joy.

"I will never, never sing at the house of this Mrs. Nevins. She has nothing in the whole world but money—nothing. She is utterly impossible. She does not even know how to patronize graciously."

"But, dear heart, you must forget her entirely. You are not doing this for her. It is for your own home land and the people you love there, for their relief."

"But there is not a single person in your company with whom I care to be seen. You have not one single artist, no one but these society girls. I would never appear with them. I am a professional."

He laughed at her vehemence and hauteur. It was as if Ptolemy had taken offense and expostulated against the privileged classes. He held her hands fast in his.

"You will, too. It will be over in no time, and I ask it for myself, Carlota. I am absolutely selfish about it. You are my Fiametta. I wrote it for you. No one else could ever sing it. You know you were its sole inspiration. And who will know you out there? It is only to lend me your wonderful voice for our success, and some day I shall see that you sing it at the grand opera. Don't you want me to win out?"

He placed his hand under her obstinate, pointed little chin. Who was it had written,

> *"her perfect, fruit-shaped chin,*
> *Such as Correggio loved to paint"?*

And her small, thoroughbred head with its close, brown curls, the splendid depth and luster of her dark eyes, the clean, fine curve of chin and throat, they were an ever-new delight to him. She lifted her lashes slowly and met his gaze with accusing eyes.

"Will—will this girl, your new pupil, sing a rôle also?"

"Surely, dear," he told her confidently. "One must throw some sops to Cerberus, three-headed monster of wealth and otherwise. She will only have the mezzo rôle of Nedda. But you will be my princess girl, singing my *Quest of Love* for love of Italy and me. And some day, when we are very rich, just we two, we will go to Italy and find your Villa Tittani with its rose-tinted walls. Would you climb them to find me?"

Carlota smiled up at him, a flash of quick mischief in her glance.

"And what of your father who lives in Colorado? Would he allow you to"—she hesitated for the word: he had not said to marry—"to go away after love quests for rose-walled villas?"

"Dad wouldn't say a word if I had produced several successful operas." Ames went over to the window and stared quizzically down at the Square. "The verdict of your family rests solely on the world's verdict first. That's the last word with Dad, success; whether you can change your dreams into reality, kind of like the old alchemist's trick with lead into gold. The difference is that, to us, it is the dreams that are more real than the consummation, eh, dear? Forget about him. Let's figure out about your costume."

"I can get both, signor," she promised demurely; "and they will be perfectly correct, I promise."

"Don't call me that. Say Griffeth, or Griff. It isn't exactly a pet name, but I rather like it. I got it from some old Welsh forbear. Listen, I know just what you should wear. Something with a straight mediæval line like the velvet gown you wore at the Phelpses the first night I met you. I thought then how much you were like some stray princess girl like Rostand's Lointaine. Remember, he called her his remote princess."

Carlota slipped aside from his disturbing nearness, and knelt by the fire to pet Ptolemy.

"But that dress was not at all royal. I shall amaze you with one truly magnificent."

He laughed at her boasting and insisted on showing her his idea of the gown, draping her with a long silken strip of piña cloth that made a train from her slim shoulders. On the shelf above the door was a brown casserole in a perforated silver stand, crown-shaped. It made a perfect coronal, Ames declared gravely, setting it down low over her curls, somewhat heavy and Byzantine, but most becoming. Dmitri came in to acclaim her, bringing with him the first potted azalea he had happened to see in the market. He set it down on the window-seat in triumph.

"See how much I love you!" he cried. "It was very heavy, but I brought it, green tub and all. Do you know why? Of course not, my poor simpletons. It is because these flowers grow wild in abundance in my native land. They are like the roses of Sharon blossoming in our mountain wildernesses, and the color is like the dawn flush, like the maiden glow in the cheeks of our girls." He regarded the plant reflectively. "It is very strange how precious a symbol of memory becomes. My heart leapt when I saw it in the window, all abloom. How do you like it?"

"I always want to kneel before flowers," Carlota said softly, as she touched the petals with her finger-tips lingeringly. "In Italy you find flowers before the wayside shrines, and I liked them better than churches. We had a shrine in a grotto at the end of the garden—" She stopped, but neither had noticed her words. Dmitri was in a fine abstract mood.

"Shrines are the proper places of worship," he stated positively. "Groves first, no mountain-tops. All philosophers prefer the isolation of the mountain-top; witness whoever thought first of Parnassus, also Zarathustra and his taste for peaks. Every heart is in reality a secret shrine where the spirit may worship beauty, truth, ideals, love, without distraction. Why are you crowned today?" He broke off abruptly to smile with a brooding tenderness over Carlota.

Ames answered for her, telling of the approaching fête and of the production of his opera.

"And at last she has consented to sing Fiametta for me, isn't that great?" He spoke with a certain carelessness that always aroused Dmitri.

"For you? And who are you?" he demanded. "You are the eternal Harlequin, the dancing, masked juvenile of all history and fiction, the necessary evil in all romance. You always win, no matter what cards Fate deals you. You play with a stacked deck, I tell you to your face, and your dice are loaded too. You are a trickster, and none may win the hand of Columbine from you. We, who are a million times more worthy of her love, we, the thinkers, the stable, faithful adorers, are not even seen by her when you flirt your rapier, and twirl before her eyes. I hate you." He turned to Carlota calmly. "Are you going to sing at this fête?"

She smiled in confusion at his earnestness.

"I feel I must because its theme is all about my princess of Castle Tittani. I am responsible for it and its success."

"What name do you think would be good for her to take, Dmitri? You know I do not even know her own to this day. It is her whim to hide it from me. I think if it were really a beautiful one, she would tell, don't you?"

"Ignore him," Dmitri told her gravely. "Names are nothing. I thank God I was a foundling. No, you did not know that, eh? There is a certain road that leads to a monastery. If I told you where it is and its name, you would not know anything about it, but it is very old, back to the Crusades, a place of sanctuary for kings and road knights alike. There is a shrine to Saint Demetra below it. I was left before it, and a brother found me and took me to the gray stone refuge. That is quite all as a basis of fact, but I weave about it the usual fantasy of desire. First, Demetra is only our pagan goddess disguised.

She is Demeter of the harvest, the mother of food for the world, the bountiful, the ever-pitiful. And I was named Dmitri. Again, always your foundling grows up, imagining he is the lost son of the king, always of noble blood. But not I, Dmitri." He perched himself on the window-seat, one arm around the azalea tub, smoking peacefully. "I like to think there were many of us, and before I came, my mother hoped to save me, the unwanted one, from the crowded life. I like to think she found courage, with my coming, to put me forth to high adventure and give me what you call 'the big chance.' So I feel brotherhood with all the world; and when I was fourteen, they put me out of the monastery with a fair education and a fine digestion. They feed you very well there. The only thing is, I was undoubtedly ruined for the seats of the mighty. A good digestion makes a man an optimist, and I was taught to choose my food wisely, without satiety. I paraphrase the prophet. Behold, as a man eateth, so is he."

"Perhaps they are all alive, your mother, and the others," Carlota almost whispered, as she leaned towards him, listening intently.

"See, I have made you believe in my fantasy, too," he smiled down at her. "Child, even if they had existed, they would have died under the sword of the Turks like all the rest. I was called Kavec by my friends later on. It has a pleasant meaning, the giver. I have not found out yet what it is I give best to the world, but you could have all I have."

"He is only trying to prove to you how selfish I am and what a high-minded mountain dweller he is," laughed Ames. "The car is downstairs and my appointment is for one. You'll go out with me to rehearsal Tuesday, Carlota, then?"

She rose with a little sigh. When Dmitri talked she forgot the inevitable tomorrow of reality.

"Have courage to refuse if you are doing it against your will," urged Dmitri. "He is merely a time-server."

"No." She shook her head, meeting Ames's anxious eyes. "I will go Tuesday."

CHAPTER XII

The learning of Fiametta's rôle was a delight to Carlota. Once she resolved to sing it at the fête, she threw herself into it with all her heart. Ames would turn from the piano and stare up at her in amazement as she delivered the difficult passages with a perfection of tone and harmony that seemed unbelievable to him, considering the training she had received.

"You will be a sensation," he told her. "The beautiful Signorita Incognita. Sounds florid, doesn't it? I want a stately, aloof name for you. Listen, at the dress rehearsal, don't be too distant with Mrs. Nevins. She really can help you if she wants to."

Carlota's fine dark brows had lifted at this, but she had not revolted. She had all of the true artist's consistency and faithfulness to a rôle, once assumed. When the day arrived, and she went out to Belvoir to the dress rehearsal in the Nevins's car, she played her part with a vivid charm and adaptability that puzzled Ames. She had her peasant's costume with her for the fête, but not the royal raiment.

Mrs. Nevins picked her way through the transformed ballroom past decorators and carpenters, more like the sprightly Queen of Trianon at her amusements than ever. Her white curly hair was dressed in high waves, her house-gown of black chiffon velvet trailing behind her, and one bewildered Pekinese dog trying to rest itself on her train whenever she paused.

"My dear Griff, it is wonderful the progress you have made!" she exclaimed. "Nathalie is completely enthralled over her rôle. Such a tender, appealing little part, isn't it? One feels she is merely the toy of fate, torn from her love by the caprice of the princess. I have spoken to Casanova of the operetta and he has half promised to come out. Such a delightful and distinguished audience for your first effort, the Italian ambassador and his wife, Ogden Ward, Count and Countess Triolini, court painter to Humbert years ago, and Count Jurka, who was court chamberlain to the unhappy Queen Sophia. The most charming and unexpected sequence of this fearful war business has been the eager willingness of one-time enemies to coöperate now in these little relief funds. We must all pull together, mustn't we, and forget now. Jurka is the handsomest thing you ever saw; looks like a Zenda hero and all that sort of thing. He is studying our relief methods for the rehabilitation of the wounded, a special mission for the exiled queen; so dear of her, isn't it?"

Carlota, sitting behind them, heard without noting the names. Her mind was on Nathalie and her assumption of authority over Ames. It was impossible for her to avoid seeing it. She had watched them together constantly. Nathalie was beside him all the time, consulting, directing, planning on every detail. She called him by his nickname with a little, indolent proprietary intonation that enraged Carlota. Yet she had kept her temper, and had sung her own rôle with ease and surety.

"Are you quite sure," Nathalie had asked her, "that your gown will be of the period and quite appropriate? It is too bad you could not have worn it today so we might be certain. You understand, of course, mamma would be only too pleased to secure exactly the right one for you if you wish."

"It is most kind of you," smiled back Carlota serenely. "I have my gown. It is of the period and suitable for the princess."

"What name did you wish on the programme? I didn't quite catch it, and we are correcting the last proof on them today."

Carlota thought quickly and gave her new name with a flash of mischief.

"Paola Roma."

"Oh, yes, you are really Italian, aren't you? How interesting! Griff told us that you had given him the little story that inspired the operetta." Nathalie's slim fingers were busy with her hair, puffing out the soft blond strands until it looked bobbed. "Of course," she added thoughtfully, "it's one thing to give the idea, but quite another to have made it a reality, isn't it?"

"I do not consider this a reality of Mr. Ames's hopes or inspiration." Carlota's heavy-lidded eyes glanced over the ballroom interior as if it had been the side-show of some carnival. "This is really nothing but a dress rehearsal from start to finish for him. The reality will be at the grand opera itself next year."

"If mamma and Signor Casanova think it worth while," Nathalie added smilingly. "It was so nice of you to come out today. Griff has talked of you a great deal but rather made you out a little tiger cat in temperament. He told us how you broke the flower jar. You mustn't have any attacks out here tomorrow night, will you? We'll all promise to make everything easy for you."

"Better to break the flower jar than to flat your B," laughed Carlota wickedly, and the girl flushed quickly.

Ames had pleaded with her for nearly fifteen minutes to beware of one high note she always missed the purity of. The quick rap of his baton called them to attention, but the sparkle did not leave Carlota's eyes, and on the way home she was silent and unresponsive.

She had planned a dozen different ways how to escape from Maria's watchfulness the following night. Almost she had decided to take the Marchese into her confidence, and beg him to coax the signora away for the evening. It could not possibly go on much longer, the deception, nor did she wish it to. She would appear for him this once, secure the triumph for him, and afterwards the visits to the Square would cease. He was too absorbed, too selfish, she told herself passionately. He was stupid, too, else he would never have been deceived by her voice. If he had loved her, he would have found out about her at all hazards. She had given him freely, all she knew of art, had even given him the theme for his operetta, and he was thankless, as Dmitri said. He took it for granted that she was a girl of the people, from the Italian quarter below the Square, when, if he had merely thought twice, he might have known, as the protégée of the Marchese Veracci that first night he had seen her, she must have been somebody unusual.

"Shall I take you to the entrance?" Ames asked, as they neared the apartment. "You are tired, aren't you?"

She shook her head.

"Stop at the subway station in the Circle. I will take a taxi over from there, and say I have been shopping. Maria is not home, anyway. She had a call from her lawyer here—" Suddenly she turned and faced him. "How did you know where I lived? I did not know what I was saying."

He took both hands in his, drawing her to him tenderly.

"Dmitri told me you were from peacock land. That is what he calls it up this way. He has a friend who knows you and gave it away."

"A friend who knows me, Dmitri?" she repeated in surprise. "But I——we have no friends here. What did he tell you?"

"Nothing at all, except that you lived in an apartment near Central Park, when I had pictured you on Mulberry or Spring, enriching the quarter with your sweetness. And I was tempted to go to the old Marchese and ask him all about you."

She drew her hands from his, shrinking from the mere mention of such a possibility, foreseeing the excitement that would follow. Maria, Jacobelli, would the Marchese deem it his duty to tell them?

"Listen to me," she said, with the somber earnestness that sat so oddly on her youth. "I forbid you ever to discuss me with any one. When I wish you to know all about me, I myself will tell you. You understand?"

"And I am supposed to bow and say the queen can do no wrong," laughed Ames. "You will tell me yourself after the fête tomorrow night. There will be a little time between the end of the operetta and the dancing. Mrs. Nevins has arranged a special little celebration for a few and I shall have to stay for that, but I'll send you back in the car safely."

"I wish you to leave me here," she said abruptly.

The car had turned into Park Avenue from Fifty-Ninth Street, and against every protest she left him, walking north towards the St. Germain, hardly caring whether he watched her destination or not. As she turned into the vestibule, the Marchese himself rose to greet her, smiling, courtly, immaculately garbed as if he had just stepped from a reception at the Quirinal. After Ames's threat the sight of him almost weakened her; and she gave him her hand in silence.

"I knew if I but waited long enough, you would surely come," he said jauntily. "And the time was not long. I have been loitering in the tobacconist's shop at the corner. There is a man whom one might talk with over the coffee-cups in any famous center of the world, Cairo, Bagdad, Calcutta, Constantinople, or a desert khan in Persia. He was a worker in enamels before the war, then a spy, and now, behold, he sells cigarettes with a good conscience to New Yorkers. An incipient seer."

Carlota was relieved as he occupied himself with his own conversation. Maria had not returned when they entered the apartment, and she threw off her velvet cloak with relief.

"I'll make us some Russian tea, just as you like it best," she promised—"slices of orange with whole cloves in them. Maria will come soon. She went to see the lawyer about the mistake on the jewels, something about the customs, I think it was."

The Marchese sat erect.

"The customs on the jewels?" he repeated. "I saw to that myself when you entered the port. There could be no possible error. Why did she not consult me first? Who is this person?"

"A friend of Mr. Ward's. Signor Jacobelli recommended him, I believe. He thought she might have paid too much, and offered to go over the list with her."

"I do not care for our friend and good patron, Mr. Ward." The Marchese's pointed mustache rose higher. "There is something sinister about him. Ah," as Carlota brought a tea-tray and set it beside him on a low stool, "so did your beloved grandmother always serve it in the terrace loggia. You have her way exactly, my child, and her lovely hands."

Carlota piled cushions beside him, and lighted the lamp beneath the tea-kettle. Then she settled herself comfortably, and looked up at him as she had so often in the days he spoke of. Always it had been the Marchese who had been her confidant.

"Don't you think that Maria is looking very tired?"

"I thought her never more attractive and charming than that evening at Mr. Ward's."

"But since then. I don't think that she goes out enough," Carlota insisted. "She is sacrificing herself too much for me. I beg her to go and she will not. She says she has nowhere to go and she knows no one here excepting yourself."

"But, my dear child, it must not be!" exclaimed the Marchese warmly. "Of course it has been for your sake that she has secluded herself here in New York. You can see what a beauty she was in her day. Signora Roma! I have heard La Scala resound with her praises, rise to her triumph! She must not feel that she is neglected or lonely, such a woman."

"Perhaps if you would only tell her. She needs some one who has known her at her great moments, don't you know?"

"Certainly I know," he reassured her. "It was quite right of you to tell me. We will have a beautiful, quiet little dinner for her to-morrow night down at the Brevoort or Lafayette, yes? Whichever she likes, and afterwards the opera. The San Remo Company is here from South America; not so wonderful as the Metropolitan, but very delightful and intimate. You persuade her for me, and then at the psychological moment, as they say over here, we will take her by storm and make her say yes."

The outer bell rang lightly.

"Don't tell her about it now," warned Carlota. "It must be done very diplomatically or she will suspect us. Telephone to her later that you have the seats and cannot take no for an answer."

After he had gone Maria took her accustomed siesta. Veracci had sought to interest her by talking of the customs matter coming up again, but she waved him from her laughingly.

"I will not talk of anything disagreeable with you. It is quite all right, merely a little formality to go through. I assured them we were not remaining here permanently and the collection belongs in Italy. Mr. Ward had insured me every courtesy there."

The Marchese had elevated his expressive eyebrows, but did not press the point. After his departure Carlota sat by the window, embroidering a headband in rose and gold thread. How was she to open the jewel chest without Maria's knowledge. And she must have them for the princess's court costume. There was one gown of gold tissue over old-rose metal cloth, an exquisite mediæval robe that lay like a web of sunlight in one of the chests. The court train was of crimson velvet embroidered in seed pearls, and with it she longed to wear the full set of the Zoroaster rubies. Since she was to be his princess before these people, she must bear herself royally for his sake.

She sighed, and laid aside her work to look down at the quiet street. Below strolled a figure she recognized, Steccho, a belated sentinel. He had lingered in the cigar-shop while the Marchese chatted to his friend, the worker in enamels. Halfway through the night he had sat with him and Dmitri in a basement coffee-house on East Twenty-Seventh Street, listening to the new gospel of optimism which Dmitri loved to spread, he who could see good in all things and believed that service is the stabilizer of humanity's caprice. Yet, while Steccho had listened and smoked, he had watched the face of every newcomer eagerly, hoping to find one fresh from Rigl. He was growing tired of playing watchdog for Jurka.

Carlota drew the curtains together as she encountered his steady, uplifted gaze. Why did this boy keep guard over her? she wondered, and slowly smiled. He did not seem a menace. There had been a look of admiration in his eyes the day he had returned her gloves to her. Jacobelli had told her she must prepare to accept homage from all, and Ames had said a friend of Dmitri's had told him where she lived. She looked out after him as he passed leisurely down the street. In all the old-time romances that she loved, there was the "shepherd in the distance," the page who caroled unseen to Kate the queen, the gondolier who dared to lift his heart to the rose that touched a closed lattice. She wondered who he could be.

Maria sighed and stirred. The telephone rang on the little painted stand, and Carlota answered it. It was the Marchese, calling the signora. She laughed softly as he spoke to her, the color rising softly in her cheeks.

"Cara mia, it is delightful of him," she exclaimed, as she hung up the receiver. "He is the most thoughtful, charming knight errant. Ah, if you could have seen him thirty years ago! The handsomest man in all Italy. He has asked us to dine tomorrow with him and go to see *The Jewels of the Madonna*. It will do you good. Jacobelli tells me you will have it in your repertoire next year."

A curious light came in Carlota's dark eyes, a tender, half-penitent light. "The Jewels of the Madonna," and she was planning how to secure the old jewels lying hidden away in the Florentine chest by the fireplace. Even though they were her own, she felt a secret, guilty thrill over deceiving those who loved her. Surely the *Quest of Love* led one far astray and alone.

But the signora was in a gaysome mood, affectionate, pliable. She would have everything en fête. Never was she so happy as when planning a new costume that should charm and bewilder. For the dinner she would wear black velvet with a scarf of Roumanian gypsy work, intricate embroidery of orange and black that seemed made for her, Carlota said, as she draped it around her statuesque shoulders.

"You should wear a heavy necklace of topaz with that, topaz and emeralds, or just topaz set in silver."

"Heart's treasure, how you know the correct touch. Get me the key of the small chest."

"But—aren't you wearing it, dear, around your neck?"

Maria smiled at her delightedly, archly.

"I find a new hiding-place for it daily, ever since I have feared it was known we had them here. Today it is in the pot of cyclamen. Yesterday I put it in the back of the clock. Am I not wonderful?"

Carlota laughed and discovered the key planted carefully in the pot of cyclamen as she said.

"Tonight you shall hide it and show if you are a good mystifier. Look in the third tray and get out the necklaces. They are in the large tray."

The lock gave rustily. Carlota sat on the floor with the tray on her lap, lifting out the old necklaces in a dream. They were heavy and old-fashioned, but set with perfect gems. She found the topaz one and hung it around the signora's throat gently.

"It is superb," she sighed. "I was very attractive in my prime, carina, but never like your grandmother. Ah, jewels were made for her as stars for the night. Here, pile them in my drawer and pick out pearls for yourself. You will wear white while you can. After thirty it is sad."

The following day dragged slowly. Towards evening Carlota suddenly pressed her cheek with one palm as she sat at the piano. It was nothing at all, she protested, a little faintness and pain in her head.

"Nothing at all!" exclaimed Maria stormily. "When that miserable old slave-driver Jacobelli is killing you! He thinks you are made of steel. You must not go out tonight. I will telephone Veracci at once and he will agree with me."

But Carlota protested the Marchese would be broken-hearted if neither of them put in an appearance. He had his seats for the opera, and had even assured her he would order special delicacies from the chef he knew they would enjoy. It would never do to disappoint him. Maria must go, at all events.

It seemed hours before the last hum of the taxicab died away in the street below, and she turned from the window after waving to Maria. She was to go immediately to bed, relax utterly, breathe deep, forget everything and sleep. She had promised compliance faithfully, and now stood hesitant, feeling herself a traitor to all their love for her and kindness. Only for this one night, she told herself, to make sure of his success and she would never go to the Square again. It was a twenty-minute run out to Belvoir once the Jamaica turnpike was reached. She ordered a taxi softly over the house telephone, and turned to the chest. Almost wistfully and regretfully she drew the key from the hiding-place Maria had let her choose, in the back of an oval silver frame that held her mother's portrait. Would not Bianca Trelango understand, more than any other, her daughter's temptation to aid her love?

"You would not think it wrong, would you?" she whispered, as she knelt before the outspread treasures from the past. Maria kept each piece of jewelry carefully separate and wrapped in chamois, the pearls in one tray, the rubies in another, and so on. The largest pieces lay in their velvet cases at the bottom, tiaras and stomachers. Carlota hunted through the chest until she found all she longed for, the rubies her grandmother had worn in "Semiramide." There were three pieces, the tiara, necklace, and heavy girdle, each set with the gems so thickly that she caught her breath with delight. The rubies were clumsily cut and needed polishing, but they glowed slumberously against the black-velvet case, and the center stone of the tiara was the superb Zarathustra jewel itself, part of the plunder of Persia. The necklace was in sixteen strands of matched pearls with a double pendant of rubies. As she stood up to try it around her neck, she let the heavy golden girdle fall to the floor.

The sudden noise startled her, and she listened, one hand pressed hard against her beating heart. The curtains were drawn at the front windows, but were up here at the fire escapes. She drew them carefully, and waited, but there was no sound, nothing but the occasional rumble of a street car over on Madison Avenue.

The telephone bell rang and she barely kept back a cry of alarm, forgetting the taxi call she had sent in. With the costumes in a suitcase and the jewels in her traveling bag, she went downstairs, whiter than usual, her eyes wide and expectant.

"Shall I take the bag outside, miss?" asked the chauffeur. He reached for it solicitously, but she held it on her lap with both hands, and leaned back with closed eyes.

"Thanks, no. Hurry, please. Belvoir, Mrs. Carrington Nevins's residence at Strathmore. It is down near the shore past the country club. Take the shortest way after you leave the turnpike. How long will it take, do you think?"

"About an hour."

As the taxi turned into Park Avenue, she leaned forward and drew the curtain hastily. Standing on the corner, with his back to the street, was Steccho talking to Dmitri. Neither had seen her, but she left the curtains down all the long, lonely way out to Strathmore, on the north shore of Long Island. Already the rubies had laid their crimson fear on her imagination, and she dreaded she knew not what from the two silent figures that lingered near her home. Was Dmitri, too, one to be shunned and doubted? Why did they seek her? She wished with all her heart that she had taken the Marchese into her confidence.

CHAPTER XIII

It was after nine when the taxi wheeled around the crescent drive at Belvoir. Carlota leaned forward, her sense of beauty thrilled at the effect of the place in the full moonlight. It was modeled exactly, as Mrs. Nevins loved to explain, after Diane de Poitiers's love cote in France, Chenonceaux.

The fête was in full swing. She did not see Ames anywhere, but told one of the footmen who approached her that she was a singer on the programme. He led the way back of the gay crowd in the flower-festooned corridors to an inner court that had been transformed into an Italian village en fête.

Standing at the head of a wide, curving staircase was Mrs. Nevins, garbed as Vittoria Colonna, the noble lady who was Michelangelo's inspiration. Nathalie stood near, a silk domino only half concealing her chic peasant dress. At sight of her Carlota caught her breath involuntarily. Even as a child she had always loved the fêtes at the Villa Tittani, and the distinguished guests who had flocked there around the grand old Contessa. Here she was merely an unknown singer, passing unnoticed through a throng of strangers. The whimsicality of it touched her sense of humor and amused her. She was indeed Fiametta, moving unknown among the villagers.

Jacobelli stood chatting with Count D'Istria, the ambassador. They were almost within arm's length of Carlota as she passed by them, unseen and unseeing, her eyes seeking only for Ames.

"You are not overfond, then, of these society theatricals?" asked the Count. "It is for an excellent object, the milk fund for Italy."

Jacobelli lifted bored, deprecating eyebrows.

"It is torture to me, but what would you? The lady has a daughter with a voice, and she will have none but Jacobelli's opinion of its quality. Therefore I come tonight to oblige. But, ah, Count, if you could but hear my genius, my star of evening who will shortly, before another season, burst into full splendor. You recall La Paoli?"

D'Istria nodded interestedly.

"Many times I have heard my father speak of her beauty and art. I have myself been to her villa during her last years. She reigned there at Tittani as an ex-empress might have done."

"She was incomparable," Jacobelli murmured contentedly. "Then possibly you may recall the grandchild whom she adored, Bianca's daughter. Her father was the young artist from Florence whom Paoli befriended, Peppino Trelango."

The Count nodded and smiled. A child with eyes such as Del Sarto loved to paint. Yes, he remembered her. Delightedly, then, the old maestro launched into the romance of the old Contessa's death, of how Maria Roma had brought Carlota to America, of the Marchese's interest in her, and how Ogden Ward had insured her success with his patronage.

D'Istria shook his head at the mention of the financier.

"I would keep her out of his reach," he advised. "She is too young to parry the advances of such a man. Mind, I admire him greatly. He is a power in the world, a very great patron of the arts if you will, but likewise, Jacobelli, of the artistes. Arm's length, I beg."

"He will be here tonight." Jacobelli scanned the crowd, his five feet five overtopped by many. Suddenly his eyes glowed with interest, seeing a newcomer enter the court enclosure. "Is that not Jurka? I have not seen him since 1915. He was here on some government work, an attaché at Washington. A very handsome fellow, isn't he?"

D'Istria did not glance behind him. Arms folded, he stood almost at attention, his lips compressed slightly, his eyes watching Mrs. Nevins as she came down the wide staircase with Griffeth Ames.

"There is the type of man whom I admire," he said. "He has life and inspiration in his face, and he walks like one who has ridden the air."

"I do not know him." Jacobelli overlooked the stranger blandly. "Casanova told me Mrs. Nevins is a collector of celebrities. This is some youngster whose operetta she is to give a little try-out tonight, his first chance. I shall leave as soon as the daughter finishes her aria."

But the Count appeared interested in the blond youngster, and merely followed with his gaze the slim, distinguished figure of the Bulgarian ex-attaché, as the latter moved through the throng.

The suite reserved for the singers and other entertainers was on the second floor. Carlota resented the line of demarcation between the professionals and the society participants, but Ames came to her as soon as he could relinquish Mrs. Nevins to Jurka. He was so happy and buoyant, she dared not say anything to curb or quell his enthusiasm.

"Forget them all, dear," he whispered to her. "Think of what this may mean for us both. I wish Casanova were here. She tried to get him, but he hates these society round-ups, and I don't blame him. Did you find your dressing-room? I got one for you alone."

After he had gone one of the maids assisted her to unpack and slip into the court costume. There was a full-length mirror in the inner door. She regarded her reflection in it gravely as the woman arranged her curls, combing them into soft full clusters around her shoulders. The deep, vivid color of the gown was strikingly becoming to her.

"You should have some jewels—" she began.

"They are all there, in my handbag," Carlota directed. As she opened the cases the maid gave a smothered exclamation of surprise, and glanced sharply at this girl pupil of Ames, who, she had heard the other servants say, had come from the Italian quarter in New York. Her experience told her these were real jewels and worth thousands of dollars.

"You will wear them all, miss?" she asked curiously, lifting the heavy stomacher of gold links, delicate as certain fragile shells.

Carlota nodded and set the tiara on her head herself. The great Zarathustra ruby in its center glowed and sparkled as if it held a heart of fire. She held out her hands for the necklace.

"Do you like them?" she asked simply, smiling for the first time at the maid. "They came from Italy and were my grandmother's."

"From Italy?" The woman straightened back her shoulders. "I am from Averna myself. You know Averna, near Roma?"

"Ah, do I not!" Carlota clasped her hands suddenly to her throat, the tears rising hot and quick to her lashes. Averna, the little tiny village one might see from the end of the gardens, Averna with its songs lifting on the evening air, and its little children clambering up the long steep rocky road, the young goats tumbling around them. "I—my home was near there, the Villa Tittani."

The woman knelt at her feet, folding her hands to her lips rapturously, and back on her feet in an instant, calm-faced.

"See how small the sea and world are," she said. "I do not work here. I am an extra for tonight, and I find a face that has looked on Averna. I know Tittani well—"

A rap came at the door and Ames's voice, calling to her to hurry. Carlota sighed, drawn back from the old days.

"Lay out the peasant dress, please, and don't forget the scarf for the head. It is hand-embroidered on old linen in red and yellow."

Before the operetta she ventured to steal out of a small balcony from the upper corridor, overlooking the inner court below. Although it was still early, they were dancing in one of the smaller rooms. She saw Ames enter with others, and recognized Nathalie even in her domino. All of the débutantes who were to sing wore them. And was it not as Dmitri warned her? He was a success with these people, she thought, wistfully. He was to reap a triumph tonight, and she had been foolish enough to risk her whole career for his, to jeopardize her future merely to make his operetta a success.

The woman from Averna had struck a chord of memory that unnerved her. She felt the lonely sorrow of Fiametta, the princess in disguise, seeking her love at the festa, and finding him only as the dancing Harlequin.

Ames sought her once more before the overture. The maid had thrown a black silk domino around her when she was ready to go down to the improvised stage, and she drew the hood closely over her head, concealing the tiara.

"All right?" he whispered confidently. "Keep your nerve, dear. It all depends on you, after all. Fiametta carries the action and sympathy."

She smiled back into his eyes in silence, compliant to his wishes, eager for his success. Nathalie pressed past them with several other girls, and laid her hand on his arm.

"We're looking everywhere for you, Griff!" she cried. "Mamma's so afraid you might forget the supper-dance afterwards. It's only for a few, and we want you to stay. Will you, just for me?"

He passed down the long stairs with them and she heard no more, but as she followed the maid down to the stage, a flood of fiery rebellion swept over her, and waiting for the music, there was the look of Paoli in her pose and flashing eyes.

D'Istria and Jurka had avoided each other by tacit mutual consent. One long look they had interchanged, and the ambassador's eyebrow had raised ever so slightly. He had given no sign of recognition, but even to Jacobelli the enmity between the two men was unmistakable. He would have been more interested in it, possibly, had not Ogden Ward arrived late, and he remained with him, telling him of Casanova's offer.

The first strains of opening music caught his ear. Ames did not call it an overture. It was not pretentious enough for that. It was merely a prelude, a mingled fantasy of Italian village-fête melodies, the harmonies that spring involuntarily from the very life-blood of a people. Jacobelli listened in alert surprise. This unknown composer had caught the secret and had woven it into his opera. He hunted covertly for his programme. The name on it, "Griffeth Ames," meant nothing to him nor did that of the soprano, Paola Roma. Had he been suspicious, Carlota's twirling about of names to suit her fancy might have given him a clue, but as it was, his professional interest in the composer absorbed him, and he passed the name by.

In the opening duet between Peppino and Nedda he suffered visibly, whispering to D'Istria.

"Ah, money, what crimes are committed in thy name! They choke art, these people; they strangle it to death with cash and coupons."

The action of the operetta was swift. Peppino had come to the castle with his daily catch. His sweetheart follows him, jealous of his admiration for the princess and his lingering in her garden. From the bower window in the tower, Fiametta watches him, and, half-hidden, hears him sing his love for her, "a certain star beyond all love of mine!" Peppino promises Nedda she shall be his choice at the festa the following day, and their betrothal announced, and she leaves, satisfied. The princess lingers in the garden after they have gone and sings "Cerca d'Amore," the quest of love.

It was on this aria that Ames based his greatest hope, and even as he led the orchestra, he sensed back of him the thrill which ran over the audience at the entrée of Carlota. He himself stared up at her in blank amazement. She had worn her silk domino up to the final moment and he had not seen her costume. But now, as she lifted her voice in the opening strains of the *Quest* song, he stared and marveled.

Mrs. Nevins lifted her pince-nez and never lowered it until the curtain fell on the interlude. Then she remarked to the woman next her in tones which demanded an explanation from Mr. Ames, "That girl is wearing a fortune in real jewels!"

Jacobelli was near-sighted. Hindered by the crowd from a clear view of the stage, the Fiametta motif did not warn him of what was about to happen, but the first notes of Carlota's voice shocked him into attention. She was singing as never before. The rôle appealed to her, the lonely little princess planning her disguise at the fête, seeking her fisher-boy love. Her rendering of the aria was a sensation. He caught a glimpse of D'Istria's face, of Ward's, and trembled with emotion. In front of him was a large, stately grande dame with opera glasses. He reached for them out of her hand imperatively.

"You permit, if you please? I cannot see. It is most imperative that I see, you understand?"

She stared at him ineffectually, but Jacobelli was far too engrossed to notice her. He had recognized Carlota through the lenses, and the color rose thickly to his face. The tragic truth burst upon him. His star had been stolen from him by this young unknown composer, his flower of genius was already plucked before his eyes, and flaunted at this miserable society fête as the pupil of another.

Even while he stood with the glasses held close to his eyes, a hand reached over his shoulder, a peremptory hand, accustomed to obedience, and took the glasses from him.

"You will pardon me," Count Jurka said gently. "It is very urgent that I see closely."

Impotently Jacobelli glared at him. The Count's face was absolutely expressionless. Possibly Georges might have guessed that his master was laboring under sudden excitement from the extreme pallor which accentuated his resemblance to a statue. Calm, youthful, and blond, he seemed the embodiment of possibly Endymion or Ganymede, a slender, effete godling, bored, as Dmitri had said, by the ennui of satiety.

Ward's face as he watched Carlota wore an amused, satirical expression. During the interlude Jacobelli started to speak to him, but was silenced by the "Hush" of those nearest him. Ames's music held society under a spell, and Mrs. Nevins was conscious of a strange mingling of satisfaction and resentment over the girl Carlota daring to appear with an array of jewels not one woman in the crowd could have equaled.

The climax of the operetta was the stabbing of Fiametta at the feast. Nathalie sang Nedda with an immature insouciance that was in character with the rôle. Peppino was sung by Jolly Allan, a young bachelor with a rich, reckless sort of voice. When he danced with the masked princess at the festa, Nedda stopped him in a jealous fury, demanding why he had neglected her. He answered with the "Quest of Love," the beautiful waltz song of the princess. Together, as they sing it, they dance, until suddenly Nedda stabs her unknown rival, and as she dies in Peppino's arms, she is unmasked and the people recognize their princess.

The curtain fell in a tumult of acclamation. Count Jurka was already bowing low over the hand of his hostess. It was with the utmost regret he must take his leave thus early. Only the opportunity of attending her fête could have brought him out from town. He congratulated her on securing the services of—ah, what was the young girl's name—Miss Roma? He stepped back to make room for Ward.

Jacobelli had broken away from the crowd, and was finding his way to the dressing-rooms beyond the balcony. Ames was already there before him, proud and joyous, forgetting everything but Carlota and her amazing triumph. At the entrance to the green and ivory salon off the balcony, the maestro encountered Nathalie, and poured forth his suspicions to her.

"This young singer, this girl, what do you call her?"

"You mean Miss Roma?" She smiled at him innocently. "Why, she's a pupil of Mr. Ames, I believe, from the Italian quarter back of where he lives on Washington Square."

Jacobelli stared at her. The memory of the duet from *La Bohème* came back to him with a jolt of pain. It had been her voice, then, that day. He had not been mistaken.

"Ah, but everybody is crazy!" he exclaimed heatedly. "She is my pupil, Carlota Trelango, the greatest coming singer of the age! Where is she? See, I will confront her. I will show him up and prove that she is my pupil."

* * * *

With her hand drawn through his arm, Ames was leading Carlota down the opposite flight of stairs into the court when she suddenly drew back.

"Please, I can't go down there," she whispered, pleadingly. "Let me go home at once. I—I am not well; I want to leave now."

Through the crowd came Ward towards them leisurely, with the abstracted air that was his habitually, but he had already seen her, and she shrank back from his amused, twisted smile that seemed to degrade all that this had meant to her. Before Griffeth could detain her, she had turned and sped back up the crimson carpeted staircase into the long salon, and there came face to face with Jacobelli.

"Ingrate!" he gasped explosively, beating the air with both hands at sight of her. He wheeled about on Ames. "You—you say you are the great teacher—the maestro, when you take my greatest pupil from me—from Jacobelli!"

"It's a damned lie!" Ames retorted shortly. "She is not your pupil. I've been teaching her for weeks, months, myself."

"But she knows nobody here in America; it is utterly impossible!" cried the old maestro. "For two years I have taught her all I know. You know not what you say."

Ames caught the glances of those around them and bit his lip to keep back the words he longed to hurl at this wild-eyed, explosive individual.

"Pardon," he said curtly. "Miss Roma is my affianced wife. Now I am sure you will give me credit for being aware of her identity."

"Listen to him!" Jacobelli's rage boiled over. He appealed to Nathalie and her little group of girl friends, to Mrs. Nevins as she approached them with Ward. "Mr. Ward, I beseech—I demand that you assist me in denouncing this impostor. Is not Carlota Trelango my pupil and the granddaughter of the great Margherita Paoli? Does she not make her début at the Opera next season under Casanova?"

Mrs. Nevins moved forward deliberately, and addressed Carlota.

"Won't you kindly end this distressing scene, Miss Roma, and leave as soon as possible? I thank you for your services."

Carlota stood an instant, hesitant and proud. Ames held the little cold hand on his arm in a close grasp. Head up, he was her champion, but it was a question now which adversary to engage first, so many assailed her. In Nathalie's blue eyes was lurking a challenging ridicule as her gaze met his.

And suddenly D'Istria appeared at the head of the staircase with several friends. He came forward into the salon and bowed low over the hand Carlota extended to him wonderingly, gratefully.

"Oh, Count D'Istria," she cried eagerly. "You are here!"

Perhaps D'Istria himself sensed the meaning of the silent group around her. He answered gently, deferentially.

"After these years, signorina, it is with the greatest pride for our Italy that I greet you tonight. The last time you were weaving chains of rosebuds at the old Contessa's knee in the garden of Tittani. Now, I find you wearing a crown of laurel on your own little head."

Mrs. Nevins caught her breath swiftly, but Jacobelli murmured over and over, pacing the length of the salon alone, as if it gave him the only inward relief, the one word:

"Ingrate!"

CHAPTER XIV

It was quarter of eleven when Jurka's car left Belvoir. Along the shore road it sped, a low, fleeting shadow lured by its own projecting rays, as if some sinister genie of the night were drawing it irresistibly on towards the city glow in the west.

The Count smoked thoughtfully, leisurely, selecting cigarettes from a black and gold enameled case as one selects favorites from a seraglio. Fate had tendered him the information he had come to America after, and he already contemplated a pleasurable return to Switzerland first, and then to Sofia with the profits from what he cleverly dubbed Love's plunder.

He had recognized them the instant Carlota had stepped into the full light. First the tiara with its splendid center ruby, the Zarathustra, and the curious Byzantine setting. The ruby was one of the three greatest in the world. It had been taken, centuries before, from a shrine of the Zoroastrians beyond the Caspian country. Slipping from hand to hand it had brought untold carnage and horror to the land whose queen wore it on her brow. Only half a century before it had been coveted by a woman of the Balkans whose ambition led her throneward. She had been maid of honor to an emotional, harassed queen, and had stepped over her dead body to wed her son. The price of the ruby had been one keen, swift knife-thrust through her heart and another for the blundering, love-blind prince. Ten years after, the ruby had been found in a Cairo curio-shop by one who knew its value, and had been sent out to seek the jewel marts of Amsterdam. It had been returned to the Bulgarian state coffers until Paoli, in the zenith of her beauty and fame, had received it from the hands of the crown prince, mounted in the tiara with other gems fit to bear it company.

The girl Carlota could not be aware of the value or tremendous significance of the rubies, Jurka reflected, else why should she subject herself to the danger of wearing them in public? Taken with the necklace and stomacher, they represented an immense sum, entirely apart from their peculiar antiquarian value. Yet she had donned them for this charity fête as if they had been paste.

Touching the mother-of-pearl button concealed in the buff suède cushions, he drew a small, black-belted card-case from his breast pocket, and opened a folded oblong of thin tracing-paper. Drawn upon it delicately was a perfect sketch of the settings holding the crown rubies. Jurka held it close to the shaded bulb, studying the detail carefully until the car approached the city.

"Choose quiet streets," he ordered through the speaking-tube. "Make haste!"

His early arrival was unexpected by Georges, and the valet stood on guard as the key sounded in the outer lock.

"Pardon, excellenza," he begged. "I did not know whom to expect."

"Find me Steccho at once. Take him in a taxi to the Park entrance at Columbus Circle. Dismiss the car there and walk into the shadows of the Park. I will pick you up a hundred yards beyond the Monument at twelve-thirty." He paused to glance at his own reflection in the long mirror, adding, as to his chauffeur, "Make haste!"

Back at Belvoir Carlota had dressed while Jacobelli paced up and down outside her door. The maid assisted her excitedly, fondling the jewels and gown as she packed them.

"You were a triumph, Miss Roma," she said. "They talk of nothing but you outside."

Carlota did not answer. Her face was pale and determined. Jacobelli had telephoned the Lafayette after demanding from her Maria's whereabouts. He had had the Marchese paged, and had asked him most sarcastically where he imagined Carlota might be at that hour. Where, returned the old Marchese genially, but in her own bed, reposing restfully, after a most severe headache?

"She is not that," stormed Jacobelli. "She is out here—at Belvoir, Long Island, at the home of Mrs. Nevins, wasting her voice for charity with a person who claims he is her teacher. I bring her back with me at once."

The Marchese protested that Carlota could not have any wrong intentions, that Maria must not be alarmed.

"Alarmed!" repeated Jacobelli solemnly. "I would so alarm her that never would she permit the girl out of her sight until her début. I tell you this is not a joke, Veracci. She has scaled the wall of Tittani, mark me. You will understand when you see this man. Meet us at the apartment. Not only has she sung here tonight, but she has wasted also the Paoli jewels. She has worn the priceless rubies of Margherita as if they were garnets."

He lingered in the corridor booth, and Ames watched eagerly for a glimpse of Carlota before she left. Mrs. Nevins was delicately, pointedly cynical and distant with him.

"My dear Mr. Ames, can't you see that this is all rather unpleasant for me? Of course the girl is very pretty and her voice is a rarity, but, after all, was it not somewhat unprofessional and unsportsmanlike of you to enter her in a race for amateurs, as it were?"

"But I never dreamt for an instant that she was from a famous or professional family," Ames denied earnestly. "I don't believe that ranting old rascal, anyway, not until I hear it from her own lips."

"No?" she smiled. "Of course I did not know she was engaged to you. But you believe Count D'Istria surely. It all places me in a most delicate situation and jeopardized the success of the entire evening. Nathalie will be prostrated tomorrow. She had such faith in you."

"But I can explain everything," Ames replied moodily. Why on earth was Carlota lingering so long when Jacobelli might reappear any instant.

"I fear the opportunity is lost, although I do not doubt your aptitude for explaining anything." She gave him her hand with a little, pitying smile. "She will be Jacobelli's pupil after tonight, Mr. Ames. If you will send me your bill for expenses and services of Miss Roma and yourself, my secretary will mail you a check. Ah, my dear boy, you were too promising a genius to have permitted a little infatuation for this girl to ruin your career."

She left him standing in the ivory and green salon, furious and helpless. At length the door of Carlota's dressing-room opened, and she emerged, slim and demure in her long black velvet evening cloak. It was made with a monk's hood falling back from her head, and as she hesitated, looking cautiously about for Jacobelli, he thought of Juliet, awaiting the return of the nurse in the garden.

Before he could reach her Jacobelli appeared, and took her resolutely under his care. Only one long look passed between them, but to Ames it was a promissory note from hope drawn on tomorrow. As he stood alone after they had gone, the Italian maid came from the room, and gave him a note, her black eyes filled with mystery.

"It is from her," she whispered. "My name is Assunta Rizzio. My home is within sight of the tower windows of hers in Italy, and I love her. You may call upon me if you need me. See, I live here."

He smiled gratefully, and crumpled the card she gave him into his pocket while he looked at Carlota's last word:

It is all quite true, but I am alone to blame. I thought Mr. Phelps might have told you, and you were but playing our little game with me, of Pierrot and Columbine. Now, it is all over, is it not? You will hate me for ruining your opera, and I do not blame you. I am sorry, it is all I can say. I thought I was helping you. Give my love to Dmitri. He was right, was he not?—and behold, the Princess Fiametta should never have left the wall of Tittani.

He passed down into the court. It was nearly empty, only the few who remained for Mrs. Nevins's private supper and dance. Ward talked with the ambassador, listening as D'Istria told happily of his memories at the old Contessa's villa. As Ames approached, he turned to him eagerly, his fine, lean face alert with appreciation.

"It was superb, Mr. Ames, a most beautiful little conception. I trust that you may have a public production before long."

The praise was unexpected, coming after the scene with Jacobelli and Mrs. Nevins. Griffeth felt almost a boyish gratitude surge through him warmly, and he thanked D'Istria with a break in his voice.

"The score is in Casanova's hands now," he told him, while Ward's gray eyes never left his face. "I had hoped he might be here tonight."

"He could not. Tonight he gives a large reception himself after the concert at the Ritz. It will give me great pleasure to draw his attention to the score when I see him, if you will permit."

With the ambassador's hand-clasp toning his new outlook on life and opportunity, Ames passed the long half-circle of waiting cars in the courtyard, and made for the station on foot. Dmitri had been right in his estimate of patronage. In the reaction he longed for a quiet talk and smoke with him beside the copper brazier.

As Carlota came into the glow of the porte-cochère's spreading light, Jacobelli took her handbag from her.

"Mr. Ward is kind enough to take you to your home," he said authoritatively. "He will be here presently."

He set her two suitcases in beside her, but she neither answered him nor even met his glance. Sinking back in the corner of the heavily cushioned car, she closed her eyes, feigning utter weariness. It was Griffeth's last look that haunted her thoughts. Would the girl Assunta give him her note. She knew that she had done wrong professionally, that she had been guilty of almost an unpardonable error, yet it was not of Ward she thought, nor of Casanova and the chance that she might lose the financier's patronage. The tender irresistible harmonies of *Cerca d'Amore* filled her brain. She could barely resist humming them, and smiling defiantly at the two moody faces after Ward joined them, and the car turned towards the city. Ward smoked small black cigars until the interior of the car was hazy with smoke and the maestro coughed irritably, but the other man paid no attention to him, merely watched Carlota. Jacobelli rambled on during the trip, but always striking the same motif.

"This to me, to Jacobelli! My greatest pupil jeopardizes her whole career by appearing prematurely at a charity fête for an unknown composer."

"I did it for love of Italy," Carlota told him with sudden passion. "If you were truly a patriot, you would be glad."

"Love of Italy!" Jacobelli groaned at her stroke of diplomacy. "Bah! Love, yes, but not for Italy. You are infatuated with this nobody, this lapper from the saucer of cream people like Mrs. Nevins sets for patronage. This is not the professional strain in you of the Paoli. This is the Peppino Trelango strain. He delighted in the silken cushion, the easy path of the rich patron. You are an ingrate!"

He folded his arms and leaned back austerely. Carlota forced herself to keep silent before Ward. He moved, shifting his position so that he might see her better. She had drawn the velvet monk's hood over her head, but every arc light they passed threw a flashing radiance into the car and showed him her pure, beautiful profile, delicately Roman, and the glamour of her near presence unnerved him.

"And those jewels which you have not the sense to value!" burst forth Jacobelli again. "I shall warn the Marchese to act at once as your guardian and place them in the safety-deposit vault. You shall not have them to play with."

"I do not want them in the vault. I shall sell them and pay you and Mr. Ward for everything and return to Italy with Maria."

"To Italy!" repeated Jacobelli dryly. "Ben trovato! With this boy here."

Ward looked with musing eyes at the bag beside the maestro.

"When you are ready to dispose of them," he said deliberately, "come to me. I did not know you were in possession of these, but I have heard of the rubies. I collect rare jewels. The Zarathustra would be brought to me by dealers ultimately, and I prefer to pay you the full price if you wish to part with it."

"I will remember," Carlota said clearly, meeting his eyes for the first time.

They left him at the Fifth Avenue entrance to his club. He made no further allusion to the rubies, and Carlota forgot them in listening to Jacobelli's flood of argument until they reached the apartment. She would throw up her career after all they had done for her, merely in a fit of pique because they objected to her throwing herself away. The Marchese and Maria had not returned.

"I shall not trust you," declared Jacobelli. "I shall guard you until they come back."

Carlota faced him suddenly, in the small vestibule, her eyes brilliant with resentment and pride.

"I prefer to be alone, signor," she told him. "I think even your authority must end here in my own home."

He stared at her in amazement, and bowed as he stepped back from the door.

"I repeat the one word which fits you, ingrate!"

The door closed, and in the sudden reaction of nervous tension Carlota sank on the low couch, her face on her arms. It was nearly twelve by the clock on Maria's desk. Surely they would come now any minute, and she would have to confess everything before Jacobelli had an opportunity of presenting his version. Somehow she felt the old Marchese would sympathize with her, he who was still a faithful voyageur along the coasts of romance, but Maria would see only the wreck of her career and her ingratitude to Ward.

The memory of him brought back his offer to purchase the rubies. She opened the bag, and drew them out on the velvet cushions of the couch. Maria had called them priceless, these glowing bits of imprisoned glory. Against the gray brocade of the cushion, their vivid, blood-red hue fascinated her, but only with the thrill at their beauty. She was like Paoli on whom they had been lavished. There was no craving in her nature for outer ornamentation, no lure from wealth or jewels. She touched them now curiously, half regretfully. Ward had said he would become their purchaser at any time when she wished to dispose of them. She rose with quick resolution and searched for his telephone number in the book. The bell rang with startling sharpness in the still room. She raised the receiver, expecting to hear Ames, but the suave, cheery tones of the Marchese sounded over the wire.

"Maria would have me call you up before we went on to Casanova's reception, to be sure you were quite all right. You are, yes? The headache better? Ah, that is good. We may be late, about two, I think. You are to rest yourself, understand."

"Oh, tell her I understand, and she is not even to think of me," Carlota exclaimed eagerly. "It was dear of you to call me up."

She hung up after the Marchese's laughing, courtly rejoinder. Two whole hours before they would return. It seemed as if Fate had opened wide the way for her to go. She called Ward's number with surety. He had not yet returned, Ishigaki informed her, but was expected at any moment. He would give him the message.

At the same moment Georges paused before a row of low red-brick buildings on East Twenty-Eighth Street, towards Lexington Avenue. They were very quiet, private-appearing residences. Narrow, one-story porches of iron grill-work clung to each, overhung with scrawny, rugged vines that defied the city soil to make them vacate. In the basement of one was a barber shop, discreet seeming and customerless. The second floor of another bore a small sign, "Bulgarian Restaurant." Each carried over its entrance bell a slip of white paper, pasted to the brick, "Furnished Rooms."

Here, then, Georges hesitated, not knowing certainly which house held the object of his quest. It was after midnight by five minutes. The lights in the restaurant burned low. A footfall down the street towards the subway station made him turn. The late pedestrian was young and in evening dress, with a raincoat flapping back in the swirling autumn wind. The air was damp and salty with the scent of the incoming tide up the East River. He started up the steps of the house next to the restaurant when Georges accosted him. Did he know where a man named Steccho lived, Ferad Steccho?

"I don't live around here," Ames replied. "Wait a minute. I'll ask my friend."

He tapped upon one of the windows opening on the narrow iron porch, and both heard the sound of a violin within, a strange, soft harmony of undertones. Dmitri sat cross-legged on his couch like a merchant in a Bagdad bazaar, his head twisted over his violin as though it had been the head of a girl he loved held in the curve of his arm.

On a stool beside the table was Steccho, brewing coffee in a long-handled copper urn he held over a brazier of charcoal. He started up at the sound of a step on the porch, but Dmitri calmed him.

"It is only Griff," he said, rising to open the door. Ames stood on the threshold, his hand on the knob. And the boy at the brazier heard him ask where Ferad Steccho lived. Before he could warn Dmitri, Georges had caught the answer and was bowing before him.

"I disturb you, I fear," he said gravely. "I merely sought an old friend."

Steccho's face was rigid with alarm and fear. The skin seemed to tighten over his high, swarthy cheekbones. His eyes were brilliant, his lips a mere line of red in the graying tan of his face.

"I come!" he responded.

CHAPTER XV

Dmitri laid aside his violin, his eyebrows lifted querulously.

"Now, why do you suppose that black-browed grenadier comes to my threshold at dead of night and scares my friend? Sit down, Griff, sit down. You shall have such a sup of coffee as you have never tasted before, purest Mocha straight from Medina in a sack. The boy was frightened, eh?"

"I didn't notice his face," Ames retorted. "God, but I'm tired!" He stretched out full length on the couch after throwing off both coats. "You are absolutely right, Dmitri. Society is the pitfall and delusion, the desert of mirages."

"It is not a success, then, the opera? Where is Carlota?" Dmitri talked with a cigarette balanced unsteadily in one corner of his mouth, and poured off the top of the coffee deftly into small cups. "You like a dash of rose or orange water, yes?"

"I don't care what you give me. I'd drink a Lethe cocktail to-night," groaned Ames. "They took her away from me, Dmitri. She isn't poor or friendless or anything of that sort. It's a damned lie. She's the granddaughter of the great Italian diva, Paoli, and Ogden Ward is her financial backer. It reeks, lad, it reeks of the commonplace, and the rose of romance is a wired fraud."

"That is very good," Dmitri responded cheerfully. "A wired fraud peddled by the fakir Hope on street corners to catch just such boys as yourself. I told you all about it and you would not listen to me. Each lover imagines he is completely original in his unique adventure when it is merely the same old rondel sung over again. She is too beautiful to doubt, but the more beautiful they are the more you should doubt."

Ames sat up, his head bowed.

"You see, the worst of it is no one will believe I did not know who she was all the time. She is the accredited pupil of Guido Jacobelli, and yet she permitted me to introduce her publicly as my pupil.

Why did she ever come down to the Square and let me make-believe teach her?"

Dmitri's eyebrows again became expressively active. He shook a few drops of orange water from a tiny glass decanter into each cup of coffee, and his next remark was apparently a diversion.

"Have you tried to pluck this Rose of Romance?"

"Oh, she knows I love her, of course. You don't have to tell those things outright when you are persons like Carlota and myself."

"Ah, to be sure, you sing it to each other; you play it in divine harmonies on the piano. I forget."

"Thank God, that is all."

"Then you have not let her carry away your heart and offer of marriage in her little gold bonbon case?"

Ames shook his head miserably. "No one will ever believe I did not know who she was," he repeated. "She merely told me that her people, her own people, were all dead back in Italy. Of course I thought she just came to me from some neighborhood around the quarter until you warned me where she really lived."

"My boy," Dmitri comforted him, "you love the indefinite. It would have dispelled the illusion to have trailed her into the bosom of her family. A family is so commonplace."

"But she always dressed simply."

"Simply? You do not recognize the art of the modiste and tailor. I have myself seen her wearing a coat or gown that must have cost all out of reason to her apparent circumstances, but I said nothing to dispel your happiness. There was also her voice, her hand, her very manner. Griff, you were blind not to see and know you entertained an angel unawares."

"I suppose she thought she was helping me, singing *Fiametta* tonight, and instead, it will ruin my whole career. They will call it an unthinkable and gigantic piece of unpardonable impudence by the time Jacobelli finishes with me."

"Stop thinking of yourself all the time. What of her?" warned Dmitri gently. "She did not want to go to Belvoir. She did not want ever even to sing in public, and you made her do it for you, you renegade. You get back to your own case. Do you not think she is suffering too?"

"If I thought she were, I'd be the happiest man alive," Ames declared fervently. "If I thought she really cares anything for me, that this wouldn't end everything, I mean."

"You mean, if she is the girl you believe her to be, she will not give you up?" Dmitri blew wavery, violet ovals into the air and sighed. "I do not envy you people who eternally seek to win your ideal, to bring it to earth, and make it domesticated, so to speak. Possibly this is the greatest thing that could have happened to either of you. You will be like the most wonderful lovers in the world—Dante and Beatrice. To me they are the greatest of all because they are divinely ideal. My dear boy, he had a wife and five children, yet he beheld her at the bridge over the Arno once, only once, in the crimson gown, and he immortalized her with his ideal love. Paolo possessed Francesca's avowal, Abelard had his memories in his cell, yet Dante, in his poverty of earthly happiness attained the empyrean following his dream."

"I know. They'll tell her all that sort of thing, too. You people who make a fetish of the immaterial, who believe that realization kills, amuse me."

"Amusement is the privilege of youth," Dmitri answered. "What you do not wish to understand or enjoy, you laugh away, but I tell you, your love, if realized, will kill the genius of you both, and you will find yourselves with clipped wings, domesticated wild swans ever yearning after the blue lanes of flight."

"Every philosopher loves the sound of his own voice better than that of any woman," said Ames.

Dmitri chuckled. "That is possible, quite possible, my friend. I wish I might call myself a philosopher, but I am a poor marksman. Philosophers are men who shoot mental shafts at the bull's-eye of truth. I have never hit the inner circle myself."

Ames drank his coffee thirstily and reached his cup for more. "Don't preach at me, Dmitri," he said bitterly. "I have come to you for straight advice, not a lot of axioms. Tell me what to do. She has gone away with Ward and Jacobelli. They will keep her from me."

"Wait patiently with confidence," Dmitri told him. "You will hear from her. Women are that way. There is some divine sixth sense that tells them of the beloved's sufferings. Stay here with me tonight."

Ames refused. The coffee had rested and stimulated him. He merely wanted companionship and the talk with one who believed in his success. Dmitri's optimism restored his own confidence in himself. He would walk on down to the Square, he said, and wait there for some word from Carlota.

"What a pity you can't sit down in this mood and improvise," Dmitri said regretfully. "This way you will only walk it off, when if you could but express it in music—ah, my friend, what we owe to the mad loves and erratic moods of genius. I drink to its suffering."

He accompanied Ames to the door and waved his hand in comradely fashion to him, watching until he had turned the corner of Madison Avenue. Then, with a quick sigh of relief, he ran his fingers through his hair and crossed the balcony to see if there was a light in Steccho's window next door. It was dark, but as his hand touched the knob it came in contact with a letter which had been stuck in the door. He went back to his own quarters slowly, and relighted the brazier to make fresh coffee. The letter lay on the black walnut stand where he dropped it. It had been mailed in New York, the outer envelope attested, but when he examined it closely he was certain there was a second envelope inside. It was so that his own mail came to him, sent on through secret channels from Sofia. He mused speculatively on the news it might contain for the boy, Steccho. He would surely return to tell him what the midnight visitor had wanted of him. Possibly this letter had been a forerunner of the visit. News from the mother and little sister Maryna, no doubt. He lifted his head listeningly for a footfall along the silent street, but none came. And he leaned over the charcoal blaze as the moments passed, with a brooding look that was the very expectancy of fear.

Through the wooded drives of the north end of the Park Jurka's car proceeded slowly. On the seat facing the Count, Steccho huddled. It was chilly in the early morning, and he was dressed scantily. The masterfulness of the other stole his vitality from him. He felt cowed and driven against his will. As they passed the penumbra of an arc light he would glance up at the handsome, easy-mannered figure opposite, his eyes filled with livid hatred.

"You have slipped a cog somewhere, I do not know just where yet, but it will come to me," Jurka said. "You have been following the girl for a month and you tell me you do not know where the jewels are. Where were you last night when she left the house wearing them?"

"I had watched all day," Steccho told him excitedly. "I was in Vorga's tobacco store on the corner in the afternoon. You can see the entrance from his window. She could not have passed out without my having seen her."

"You lie! You were with Dmitri Kavec. He is a known spy of the Internationals. Did you meet him in Sofia?"

Steccho closed his lips stubbornly. Dmitri was his friend. The car sped through a curving roadway round the base of a rocky precipice surmounted by an old blockhouse. In the darkness the locality lost all semblance of city scenery and might have been in the mountain fastnesses of Bulgaria. Jurka leaned forward with careless interest, and took note of their surroundings. "It is like the road to Monastir," he said, half to himself. Steccho's eyes stared at him through the gloom of the car's interior like those of some wild animal held in leash. His mother had named it "The Trail of Tears," that road from Monastir, where the weak and young had fled in the great retreat, and had been trampled to death, or had lingered for the slower fate from starvation. He himself had seen the babies, the young girls, the old people—and the memory was a veritable glut of butchery. Yet this Count smiled as he mentioned it as though it had been some tryst with pleasure which he had kept along that road from Monastir. And while the boy's thoughts leaped from one avenging plan to another, the Count continued:

"I think you lie, Steccho. Perhaps you have lied to me from the beginning. Perhaps, like Dmitri, you are a Czech spy. Do you know why he is here in America?"

"I know nothing about him," Steccho asserted, with a touch of bravado. "We were friends in Sofia. Both students at the University. I did not even know he was a spy. I had hoped he could give me news of my people."

Jurka touched the bell and the car stopped short under the overhanging shadow of autumn foliage, and as the faint light from an arc lamp up the road reached the interior, Steccho saw the round bore of a revolver facing him, held steadily and easily in Jurka's hand as it rested on his knee.

"I could kill you now and have your body thrown in the bushes yonder. It would be one way out. When I saved your life you gave in return certain assurances of faithful service."

"Ah, but you promised me you would provide safety for my mother and sister," Steccho broke in eagerly. "You hear from them, yes? I hear they have killed all the girls two years ago, cut their throats, thrown their bodies in wells, that they took them up to the mountains for the soldiers. Was Maryna among those, excellenza?"

"I have given you my word for her safety," responded Jurka. "The war is past. You brood too much over fancied terrors. Listen to reality. This is what you may fear. If you do not procure the jewels from this girl tonight, I will have your throat wrung for you like a dead fowl. We save bullets for men, not cowards."

"And after I get them, we go back, excellenza?" There was almost a whine in the query. The boy shrank back in the corner of the car. His cigarette had gone out. His face looked narrow and pinched in the darkness. "You will see that I go back to Rigl?"

"Rich for life," Jurka assured him languidly. "You will be able to buy the yellow castle, if you fancy it, and many cattle and sheep. The queen is not one to forget such services, my Steccho, nor I. When I meet her in Switzerland and give her the jewels, I will tell her of you."

The muscles of Steccho's face relaxed. After all, he was a fool to doubt. It was all quite simple. He would get the jewels. There would be the journey back as they had come, Georges as the Count's courier, he as groom, caring for the two riding-horses, Vriki and Etelka. Then the heaped-up honors from the exiled queen herself, and, yes, the yellow castle if the little tired mother and Maryna still fancied it.

The Count spoke to Georges through the tube. "Drive to the east entrance nearest Sixty-Fourth Street," he ordered. "Stop inside the Park."

He did not speak again until they came to the entrance. As Steccho swung down to the pavement, he nodded to him with debonair, care-free grace. The car turned down Fifth Avenue and Steccho paused at the corner to catch the last glimpse of it. Jurka had hummed a few bars from a favorite waltz back in Sofia. The tune touched the chords of memory and home longing as nothing else had done. It was a waltz of the people played often at the little village dances where he had met Katinka. As he walked east on Fifty-Ninth Street he remembered her as he had seen her kneeling in church, bathed in the long glow of purple light that flowed through the stained-glass aureole of Saint Genevieve. Always as he had followed Carlota from the very first she had reminded him of his dead sweetheart. Over and over, when he had been tempted to betray her visits to Ames's studio, the words had been checked on his lips as he met Jurka's eyes and remembered the day his excellenza's soldiery had carried the body of the girl from his quarters above the inn.

Twice before he reached the Saint Germain he stopped dead short, and looked back. But the lure of the yellow castle drew him forward, and he finally faced the east, eager for the night's work.

CHAPTER XVI

Ward pushed his chair back from the table, lighting a cigarette from the match Ishigaki held towards him.

"Miss Trelango's call came about half an hour ago?"

"At five minutes past twelve." The Jap gave the time with exactness. Ward's face was inscrutable.

"Get the car around. I shall want only you with me, tell Daniels."

As Ishigaki left the room he stood smoking, a half smile on his lips. In all probability tonight he would secure the Zarathustra ruby and its attendant collection. Jurka, the Bulgarian he had met at the club, had been after them, too, he remembered. He had been at the Nevins fête and had seen them. Palmieri had ascertained that the collection had been declared by Maria Roma as the personal property of Carlota Trelango, a minor non-resident alien. This much his own agent had found out. What Jurka knew, he had no idea, or his object in seeking the rubies. Was he, too, infatuated with the girl herself, and used the jewels merely as a blind to his own pursuit of her?

He drew three opals from his pocket and tossed them like dice before him on the polished surface of the table. They were perfectly matched and had come from the lacquered cabinet of the old empress whose life-span had bridged the gulf from the rice-fields along the Yang-tse to the peacock throne at Pekin. He gazed down at their changing luster musingly. Carlota had been in her most alluring mood when he had spoken with her on the telephone after Ishigaki had delivered her message. Spirited, combative, aloof, as he liked her best. The temple chimes in a corner recess sounded the half-hour. She had said she was alone. Always, in his experience, every woman had her price. As he swept the opals up in his hand at the Jap's low voice, he knew there could be no compromise now. She had dallied along the highway of romance and had found the love of youth awaiting her. Remembering the look of perfect understanding and faith between her and Ames as she had passed by him on the arm of Jacobelli, Ward felt a conscienceless determination to compel her to take his terms that night. She could do without the Paoli gems. Possibly, it might be a rather suitable tribute, later at her début, for him to present her with the necklace. He glanced into the tall Florentine mirror as he folded his scarf beneath his cloak, and followed Ishigaki to the car at the curb. The boy had only youth and ambition as assets after all.

In her apartment Carlota had deliberately set the stage for his reception. Slipping off her dressing-robe, she clad herself in a straight-cut evening gown of chiffon velvet, ranging in color from palest mauve to deepest rose, with long swaying sleeves of silver metal cloth. Her face was paler than usual, her eyes brilliant as she switched off the lights in the apartment, leaving only the one in the hall and a spray of rose globes beneath a silken shade at the head of the couch.

Kneeling before the gas-logs, she opened the leather bag to look alone for the last time on the rubies. Behind her a window opened widely to the keen night air. Once she raised her head, startled at a sound that seemed to come from the balconied fire escape. The wind blew the curtains toward her. It was dark outside. The city was sinking into a few hours of sleep before the rattle of daybreak noises. As she rose to look out of the window, the outer bell rang lightly. Standing flat against the stone wall of the building, not half a yard from the room, Steccho checked his leap, listening. If he were discovered now, they would snare him, no matter what he told. Who would believe, unless perhaps the girl herself out of the grace that was in all women, that he had not come there tonight to rob her, but to warn her, to defraud Jurka—not of the jewels, but of the slender, young purity of this child woman who had eyes like Katinka. If he could save her, could keep her for the boy who loved her, Dmitri's friend in the Square, then perhaps in some great, merciful way the knowledge of it would come to that unseen Power for good which Dmitri held still ruled the world of men and women in spite of the sea of crimson. Perhaps it might be they would save his mother and Maryna, these unseen forces, without his bargaining away his soul and life with a man like Jurka.

"You are still alone?" Ward's eyes followed the lines of her figure as she moved away from him. The changing silver and rose of her gown reminded him of the opals.

"Maria has gone with the Marchese to Casanova's reception. They telephoned they would be back about two. We have not very much time, you see." She drew the jewels from the bag and laid them before him on the round inlaid table at the head of the couch. The rose light shone on their beauty almost hungrily, catching the varying gleams from the deep red hearts of the rubies. "They are all there, all that I wore tonight, the tiara, the necklace, and the girdle. They are worth enough quite to pay you back for all you have given me, are they not?"

He looked at them quickly, and turned back to her as she stood beside the table.

"I will give you my check for two hundred and fifty thousand. The Zarathustra alone is worth half of that. You would find it out if I cheated you, and hate me afterwards. I, too, hate a cheat."

Something in his words and tone made her motionless, chilled and tense. She met his eyes challengingly.

"You mean that I am not keeping my bargain, Mr. Ward. But it was not a fair one that you made. You asked the impossible."

"That you would not get into any affairs until you had made your success." He cut her short sharply. "I was right. Tonight proved it. Left to yourself you have made yourself a laughing-stock. You ruined your own début for the sake of this fellow Ames, and smashed his career by branding him an impostor."

"I do not believe it. Count D'Istria—you yourself heard him when he spoke to me—he would not have recognized me and praised the opera if—if I had ruined him—Griffeth. You cannot kill art like that, not when it is real."

"You have the patter of his crowd at your tongue's end," sneered Ward. "You would have nothing to do with me when I offered you my love that night at dinner. You were insulted and fiery as some menaced nun, yet you meet this Ames in his studio secretly and carry on an affair with him brazenly, merely because you think you love him. Do you believe that love is its own law, then?"

And Carlota, thinking only of the old rose-tinted wall that bounded the domain of her dreams, closed her eyes and smiled.

"It is the highest law," she answered.

"So?" His arms closed about her like a vise as he crushed her to him. "I take you at your word. Do you think that I, Ogden Ward, would be such a damned fool as to let another man take you or anything else that I wanted away from me? Did you think you could throw me a few jewels like bones to a dog, and call our deal off? I want those rubies because they are like you. They are all fire and blood and passion, and I'll have you both."

He stifled the scream on her lips with one hand, lifting her on one arm easily while she fought like a captured wild animal. The table overturned behind her, and the jewels slipped to the rug as the electrolier broke its rose globes over them. The room was in darkness as he felt her suddenly relax limply in his embrace. Her hands and lips were cold, yet he told himself he had not hurt her badly, merely the pressure on her mouth to keep back the alarm. As he laid her on the couch Steccho's curved Turkish blade caught him under the left shoulder blade, and he rolled backward, reaching blindly into the darkness as he fell.

The boy waited a few moments, ready for another thrust, but there was utter silence in the room, and he drew a deep soft breath of relief. Kneeling, he gathered up the jewels carefully, without haste or dread, placing them in his inner coat pockets, the necklace with its priceless pendant next to his body where it was safest, the tiara curving under the belt at his wait, the girdle looped like a pet serpent in his pocket. Something else had fallen where the firelight caught its sparkle. He picked up one of the old empress's opals and smiled over its perfect beauty. This might please Maryna.

Before he passed back out of the window, he bent over Carlota. She lay as if sleeping, with spent, broken breathing. Ah, he would have taken her as a wolf, even as Jurka himself, this man who lay at her feet, but not now, not after the stroke he had learned in Rigl. She was safe, quite safe to leave alone with him. He lighted a cigarette calmly, buttoned his raincoat close around his throat, and swung out of the window and down the fire escape.

Those who place faith in the symbols and cabals of coincidence might have traced a triangle at that moment with Steccho at one point, Dmitri's room the apex, and the other the unlighted studio where Griffeth sat by the open window, staring out at the Square. The Bulgarian felt oddly exhilarated now that he had made his get-away safely. He paused at Fifty-Ninth Street and Madison Avenue, like a racer, sure of his victory, resting at the first lap.

It had been strange, fate forcing the possession of the rubies upon him. He was fatalist enough to accept. And it would be better for the girl Carlota. They would find her in time. Ward had terrified her, but she was unhurt, he felt certain, except for the marks on her throat. He looked back over the way he had come. There was no sign of alarm yet, no shrill blowing of police whistles, nothing but the customary flow of crosstown traffic at that hour. He bought an early paper, and took a car bound downtown. The jewels themselves reminded him, as he touched them in his pockets, that he had not failed when the hour of fate had struck for him. He bore the wealth of a rajah on his body, and the knowledge gave him a suppressed braggadocio as if he had picked up life's challenge and had won his first prize in the lists of opportunity. If only the girl, as she lay there, had not looked like Katinka, more like her than ever with the pallor and look of pain on her face. He shook off the sentiment and focused his attention on Jurka.

He had given him until morning. Good; then he should have the jewels three hours before dawn. Georges's black eyes would show smouldering fires of envy when he, Ferad Steccho, carelessly poured forth the missing rubies from his pockets, the rubies of the queen, as if they had been pebbles. Doubtless another night, and they would all be on their way back. He shut his eyes, half imagining the lurch of the car was the first roll of the ship as it touched the deep sea, and the far-off city noises were the distant surge of ocean waves.

True, there would be an outcry when they found the body of Ward, but there was no one to tell who had stabbed him. The girl had been unconscious. His eyes narrowed suddenly. Would they, then, possibly accuse her? Would Ward, if by any chance the blow had not killed him, dare to revenge himself on her by swearing that she had stabbed him?

As the car reached Thirty-Fourth Street he shook off the depression and made direct for the Dupont, confident of his welcome. There was no response, he was told at the desk. He demanded that they call the Count's private room. It was impossible, the clerk told him. Count Jurka's orders were he was not to be disturbed. Would he send up a card with a message? He shrugged his shoulders, and wrote rapidly in Bulgarian:

They will not let me up to you. Send Georges at once. I fancy the yellow castle, excellenza.

The triangle of coincidence had become an isosceles. He walked over to Lexington Avenue, and walked down to Twenty-Eighth Street, taking his time, his usual surliness settling in a fog of resentment over his mood of happiness. So he must wait, wait while the Count had his unbroken rest, while the workers, the doers, waited on the whims of such as he like dogs on doormats. Well, they might come to him now, to him, Steccho, if they wanted the jewels. He would go to Dmitri's room and stretch out by the fire and sleep the hours before daylight. He had not touched food since the previous day, nothing but black coffee and cigarettes. The plan struck him with pleasure, as a sort of revenge on Jurka. He would not tell Dmitri what he had done; merely sit and chat with him to prove he did not do the bidding of the Count.

When he mounted the steps of the red-brick house with the iron railing around its balcony, there came the low sound of violin-playing from within. Dmitri then was still awake. His grate was ablaze with a good fire of boxwood and charcoal. His coffee waited the whim of his desire, over the unlighted brazier. Meanwhile, he said hello, as he expressed it, to his consort, "Madame Harmony."

"Behold, she never deserts me," he would say to Ames. "She is the most patient yet alluring of mistresses, my madame. And when I caress her, ah, what she tells to me!"

There was no pathos in his music tonight. A Czech folk-dance spun from his fingers in curling, whirling, leaping strains of melody like some strange, intangible confetti of vibration expressed in notes. The lure of it held the boy and he waited in the doorway, his dark eyes filled with a passion of home yearning. So often he had danced with her, Katinka, to that same music. At the instant some one on another street blew a car whistle, and he slammed shut the door, locking it with shaking fingers.

CHAPTER XVII

"Now what?" demanded Dmitri cheerily. "You look as stark as a dead fish, my friend. Have some wine."

Steccho took the full glass gratefully, drained it, his head thrown far back, and wiped his lips with a sweep of his hand.

"I thought it was the police," he said unsteadily.

Dmitri lit the fire in the brazier before he spoke. His eyes were filled with brooding solicitude when he looked back at the boy. Steccho's whole posture showed more than mere exhaustion. There were dejection and fear in the slouch of his body as he sat forward on the edge of the couch, his fingers crumpled in his hair.

"You have done something tonight?"

The boy nodded.

Dmitri measured powdered Arabian coffee into the copper pot carefully.

"It is a pitiful penalty of wrongdoing," he said compassionately, "the little ghosts of fear one must forever entertain. You have been followed here?"

"I am not afraid. I am hungry." A shudder like a chill shook his narrow, stooped shoulders. Dmitri eyed him anxiously. "Let us go around to Barouki, some place where it is quiet and we can talk."

"None better than here. Lay off your coat and lie down. I will have you such a meal in twenty minutes as you have not tasted in months, not since you left home. I have broth, wine, and lamb to broil; grapes and bread and coffee." He set a pot of broth over the blaze, brought out lamb from the cupboard with a small, smooth board to cut it on, and sat cross-legged on the floor before the brazier while he cut the meat into slices and skewered it with slices of raw onion between. "I am no wanderer at heart, you see. I like my own hearth-fire even if it is merely a charcoal blaze like this. I prefer to cook my own meals and know what I feed upon. Drink that broth."

Steccho obeyed in moody silence. The reaction had set in after his rebuff at the Dupont. He drank the broth in deep swallows. The peace and genial atmosphere of the room had begun to seep through his consciousness as it always did. He felt that here he might lie and sleep for hours, until the fear that dogged his heels should have lost the scent. He wondered if the blade had reached the heart. He had dropped without a cry, the man who desired both rubies and her who was more precious than rubies. If it had not killed him, then he would waken and accuse—whom would he accuse? He had seen no assailant in the darkness. Would he, perhaps, say that Carlota had stabbed him, would he dare when he knew she had been unconscious in his arms? Besides, they would discover the rubies were gone; that would prove she was innocent, that another had dealt the blow and had taken them. He yawned exhaustedly.

"You could hide me here, if it had to be, yes?"

"Doubtless." Dmitri set a savory mess of browned lamb on the black oak table and poured boiled rice into the broth to simmer. "I could hide you, but you would have to tell me why you were hiding. In these days we must guard our friends against their own impulses. Whom have you killed, Ferad?"

The Bulgarian stretched out his palms excitedly.

"And what is that, the death-stroke, nowadays? Life is the cheapest thing in the world."

Dmitri poured wine into two tall metal drinking-cups. From the Metropolitan Tower came the strokes of two. He served the rice in silence, reserving comment, waiting for the confidence of the other. And suddenly Steccho rose from the table. He had eaten with a ravening hunger; now his old air of sullen bravado returned. He turned pocket after pocket inside out, emptying the jewels on the table before Dmitri as if he had been a gamin rolling marbles. Dmitri lifted his brows in relief and amusement as he looked at them, rubies and diamonds, rubies and pearls, set in old silver and gold.

"So, you play with these, my friend," he smiled. "I had thought you were grown to a man's desire. These are the devil's toys to catch the tinkling fancy of women and girls. Did you need money? I would have given you all I had."

Steccho laughed, his heavy black hair rumpled over his forehead. He shook his head impatiently. After his long fast, the wine was stirring his brain to resentment against Jurka.

"I bring them to you that you may choose for me," he said. "This is why I am here. They are the missing crown jewels, the rubies of the queen."

Dmitri stared at him incredulously. Yet the gems lay there before him. The boy spoke the truth. These were imperial in their beauty and value. He lifted the pendant, gazing intently at the Zarathustra ruby, the second largest in the world.

"The queen?" he repeated incredulously. "She is in Switzerland. She sent you here?"

"Not I." Steccho laughed in derision, tightening his belt. "I am Ferad Steccho, a dog to be kicked and denied, you understand. The queen will thank Count Jurka, but I—I, Steccho, am the one who got the jewels for her, and it is you, my Dmitri, who will decide whether we ever give these to the queen who waits for them. That is why I come to you, not to hide me, but to tell me what to do."

Dmitri's thoughts centered on the name he had spoken, Jurka. The former court chamberlain, the ex-attaché who had been given the favor and confidence of the queen herself in the cataclysm of fate that had swept her throne from under her, the suave, faithful, blond Jurka. He watched the dark, eager face of the boy, touched with vivid high lights along point of chin, cheek, and nose by the firelight in the open grate.

"Do you think for one moment a man like Jurka would undertake this mission out of any loyalty or desire to assist a queen in exile unless—I did not think you would help to feather the nest of such a bird as Jurka."

He checked himself abruptly. Steccho struck his clenched fists upon the table between them, the jewels unheeded as he poured out his words.

"I did not take them for him or for the queen. It was the price he demanded of me for the safety of my mother and sister."

Dmitri glanced to the mantel where the letter lay. He had forgotten it in the surprise of Steccho's coming, but now he waited to hear him out before he gave it to him.

"Jurka sent for me in Sofia. He was working with the relief committee there, a mask to hide behind merely. He remains an agent of the royalists. He told me these were part of the crown jewels. They had been stolen years ago by some Italian woman loved by the crown prince. He said they had traced them here to New York. What do I care for them?" He pushed the rubies from him resentfully. "I tell you they are unlucky. The rubies are for blood, the pearls for tears, always I hear my mother tell that. Here they were worn by an innocent girl—"

He stopped. Would he tell Dmitri all the truth, of the girl Carlota, whom his friend had loved, of her peril, and why he had taken the jewels from the keeping of the man who jeered at love?

"How did you first meet Jurka? How did he know these were here? Whom have you killed to get them for him?"

Dmitri strove to speak calmly. Behind the boy's story lay some conspiracy of Jurka's, another undercurrent to reckon with in the great crimson tidal wave.

"I was suspected of being a revolutionist and ordered shot." Steccho spoke jerkily, between his teeth, his head back as he smoked. "My father was head gamekeeper, before the war, on the Count's estate north of Rigl where our home was. You know the place? On the mountain road from Moritza there is a castle of yellow rock standing high above the town." He drew long inhaled puffs from his cigarette. The castle in the sun glow! The strange, numb, unsteadiness swept over him again as it had back there on the fire escape when he had watched the man seize Carlota. Lust and youth, even as Jurka had ravished the sweetness and laughter and pure joyousness of Katinka.

Dmitri and the room slipped out of his vision, submerged in a gray ocean of restfulness beyond which gleamed the castle of his dreams. How it had stood as an eternal symbol to his boyhood of the pomp and majesty of kings! Then had come the schooling at Sofia, and the smouldering fires of revolution that crept through the dry rotting underbrush and mould of oppression, unnoted by those who saw only the bravery of waving green boughs in the sunlight.

He had met Dmitri Kavec there, a teacher of political economy and sociology, tutoring younger men to pay his way, writing for certain Continental papers, talking always of the day when freedom should dawn. He was a Czech, with a mingling of Romany blood in his veins. It showed in his mastery of the violin, in his dark skin, not swarthy like Steccho's, but clear and pale as yellow wine with the underlay of red. The boy's eyes were furtive, restless, Dmitri's like those of some captive eagle that sits motionless, watching passing crowds, alert and fearless. He, Steccho, had felt proud when he had been asked to join the group of men who assembled nightly in Dmitri's quarters above the old coffee-house in the lower square. He had sat and listened to them, learning much of the underground wiring of secret diplomacy, much of the patience of the thinkers and workers.

Then had come dissension and a break in the university club ranks. Dmitri was called a dreamer, one of those who believed the end might be reached by brotherhood and teaching of the people. Even Steccho had chafed at such doctrine. Rather he liked the fighting, the carrying of blazing flambeaux in the race, the song of the torch, as Dmitri called their propaganda. After the outbreak of war he had become a spy for the Internationals. It had ended with that winter day when the royalist troops had caught him hiding in Rigl. A troop occupied the town on its way up to the mountain passes above Moritza. Personages of importance sat in conference with Jurka in the old smoke-stained room at the inn, and Steccho had found a way of listening, half-wedged down the side flue of an old rock chimney.

He had overheard much, gossip mostly from Jurka, of the vacillating, ambitious king who craved the title of Czar, of his wife, the sour-visaged queen, whom he had never loved, the stool pigeon of William. They had chatted of these, speculating on who would head the royalist cause if some day Ferdinand chanced to oversleep, found like his old friend Abdul Hamid with a five-inch blade parting his ribs.

Steccho had listened eagerly. There was a trickle of truth here and there through the talk. They placed more confidence in Sophia than in the king. The soldiers were grumbling for back pay. Some officers had been shot in the back by their own men. They had been caught fraternizing with the enemy, exchanging food and tobacco under the very noses of the nobles. Stores of supplies for the officers' mess had been broken open and scattered to the wounded by their comrades.

Straws in the wind, Jurka said, his back to the fireplace, but signs to the wise. The people wearied of oppression. They must be taught to dance to a new tune. With victory Bulgaria would swallow up her enemies, she would sit like a brooding lioness, her cubs about her, renegade Greece, recreant Roumania, Servia crawling, the Slovacs whipped to heel. And eager to hear more, Steccho had leaned like a fool too far forward to catch the low-spoken words, and a rumble of loosened bricks had startled the soldiers into action.

He had been forced down by a dozen pricking, reaching sword-points as if he had been a porcupine in a hole, and had been condemned to be shot at once against the stable wall in the courtyard below.

He had heard the scream of his mother as the old women held her back, and had tried to reach her. The soldiers had beaten and kicked him as he lay in the snow, and Maryna, the little sister, had burst through the line, and by some miracle of grace he had been granted his life at her plea. Jurka had said with grave gallantry, as he smoothed back her heavy silken flaxen hair, that Saint Ginevra herself had surely intervened in his behalf.

"So you became a royalist, a serf—rather than join the gray marchers to the shades?" Dmitri smiled at the boy. "Better to have remained up the chimney and wakened singing in a chorus of victory. See how your hand shakes. You have bad nerves, my boy. You rush down here in a fit of pique like an emotional girl because Jurka desires to sleep and not be disturbed. If he refused to see you tomorrow, you might throw the playthings into the river and become revolutionist again. That way lies madness."

Steccho picked up the necklace, staring at the rubies with dreamy eyes. The warmth of the fire and the good meal with wine filled him with a glow of relaxed nerves and a sense of well-being and safety.

"I am no revolutionist. I hate to kill. I hate strife and turmoil and change. Yet I hate Jurka, too, and his kind. I was his bondman because he swore to protect my mother and Maryna. Do you know what they did after the uprising in Poltenza, twelve miles from us? They shot the villagers down against the gray wall of the market-place, two hundred of them, and the girls were given first to the officers, then to the soldiery, and we found their bodies piled in the wells, a trick from the Turks. It serves two purposes. We have been patient, Dmitri. See, I ask you. Shall we sell these and give the money to those who work for freedom? How much could I get for them, two hundred thousand, three, five?"

"More," replied Dmitri gently, "and your throat slit. Listen, my boy. Revolution is a mad dog. Who will thrust a lighted torch into the hands of a maniac or idiot? I do not think the hour has struck when men are content with the creed of violence. They weary of bloodshed. They ask, Is this all, bodies, bodies, more bodies until the whole horizon is filled with them, and one may not find the sky?"

"Ah, you talk," Steccho muttered drowsily. "Jurka says you are a spy of the Internationals."

Dmitri smiled, slowly stirring the charcoal embers beneath the brazier into a glow.

"I am no spy," he said. "I am a watcher on the outer walls, my Ferad. I am an opportunist, not aristocrat nor socialist nor even democrat. I do not like a beaten path, but I love the ideals of tradition. I love opportunity. That is why America fascinates me. Life is a game, and all games lose their zest if one plays with a cheat, he who ignores the rules and sets up his own. One objects to the stacked deck and loaded dice. Also, each man should have a chance to deal. The trouble with your Jurkas, your aristocrat, he deals all the hands and gives himself the best. The trouble with you revolutionists, you would deal everybody the same kind of a hand, and that makes the game stupid and uninteresting. There is no law of chance, no thrill to your game. You fatalists believe that man deals, but Fate shuffles the cards. Have more to eat."

"No one can play a fair game with such as Jurka."

Steccho ignored the proffered food, his face on his hands.

"Then use his own tricks against him. Look you, my friend, the gambling instinct is the keenest in all men, for we have learned that, after all, life is a great gamble. The only thing you are sure of is that you are sure of nothing. If I took up this sport, this gambling with human lives, I would do so for the pure thrill of it. I like the plunger, the good loser always. But your Jurka type, he who plays the game doggedly, who merely wants something for nothing, you will find him a bad loser. He plays to win only; the other type of man plays for the thrill of achievement. Your anarchist, too, he takes a hand. If he loses, he will say the game is crooked, and demand a new deal. If he wins, he plays safe and stops, taking all the winnings. He is like your aristocrat, after all; he will amuse himself with solitaire forever if you give him the chance."

Steccho rose moodily, walking up and down the floor.

"You have stolen to please the lust of empire," Dmitri resumed, smoking leisurely. "You are like the man who is afraid to play the game, to take a chance himself, so he turns the wheel for others. If he fares well from the man who wins, he likes him; if not, then he is for the man who loses. He listens to what this man says, Let us break up this house and do away with gambling forever. We will all play safe, then, eh? But it is not possible, Ferad. All philosophy fails to reconcile human nature. We are all gamblers. The trouble is that your Jurkas give the game a bad odor, and then the losers cry out that the whole game is not worth while. We are too selfish. We forget that we all lay up riches but for the heirs of tomorrow. I would make the way easy. I would strive to clear away the barriers that all might reach the goal of opportunity. Yet I would not hobble the swift that the slow may keep pace with them. Will you sleep here tonight?" He laid his arm around the boy's shoulders. "Do not think me unsympathetic. It is dangerous to play the game here, and the weak go under. There are some that cheat. I think Jurka is a cheat. We did not fight to make the world safe; that would be a bore. We fought to make it livable."

"I do not care for anything but to see my mother and sister again," said Steccho.

Dmitri's brow cleared. "Ah, and I am forgetting all the good news for you!" he cried, seizing the letter from the mantel. "Here is word from home. We will pour more wine and plan to send you back free from the talons of the black eagle."

Steccho's face softened in a glow of tenderness as he caught the letter. There came the noise from without of a footfall on the steps, hesitant, doubtful. As the boy swept the jewels from the table, a tapping sounded on the outer door. Dmitri flung back the drapery before the door of his bedroom.

"There is the window," he whispered. "Watch out before you drop from it."

The knock came again, this time louder. He lowered the light and went to answer it.

CHAPTER XVIII

Carlota stood on the threshold. Her face was white in the semi-darkness. In the east a faint quiver of radiance showed in the sky like the reflection of moonlight on dark waters. Dmitri stared at the girl in wonderment.

"I want Griffeth," she said eagerly. "I went to his house and he has not been there. Oh, I must see him, Dmitri! Tell me he is here with you!"

The underlying note of intense repression in her voice struck him, and yet he hesitated, fearful of Steccho's safety.

"He is not here. He left after midnight. Are you alone, my dear?"

"Surely I am alone; what do you suppose I came for? Would you rather I went first to the police? I came to you because you are his friend and I need him."

She brushed past him into the narrow hallway. He almost smiled at this twist to Griffeth's romance. With all the ardor and recklessness of her temperament and race, Carlota had flung discretion to the winds and had come to seek the man she loved at all hazards. Once inside his door, she let her cloak slip from her shoulders and stood in the center of the room, a slender, isolated figure.

"You are all afraid for yourselves," she said slowly, scornfully. "Even you, Dmitri, with all the brotherliness you profess, think only of yourself. Griffeth will not be like that. He will understand that I never can go back there."

"You are excited and nervous." Dmitri took her cold hands in his with the whimsical, cheery way that never failed to soothe. "Why should you go to the police? Tell me what has happened. It is surely a night of witchcraft when foul fiends prowl. So, now sit down and be very calm. I can always make you smile, with my nonsense, you see?"

She tried to meet his eyes, but her own filled with tears and she bit her lip to keep control of herself.

"Oh, Dmitri, I am frightened, after all. Did Griffeth tell you about the fête at Mrs. Nevins's and—and how I had deceived you both, when you were so good to me? I only sang for his sake, so his opera would surely be a success. I never dreamt that any one would be there who would recognize me; you believe me, don't you?"

Dmitri lit a fresh cigarette with musing eyes, tossed away the match, and hummed Fiametta's motif softly under his breath.

"So you yourself have scaled the castle wall to seek your love," he said. "Did they try to hold you from him?"

"It is worse than you can think, Dmitri. Tonight when I returned there was no one in the apartment. I called up Ogden Ward; do you know him?"

Dmitri's level eyebrows contracted at the name. He eyed her oddly, remembering Griffeth's words that the banker had been her patron.

"I know him; what then?"

"He was stabbed in my apartment a little while ago," she whispered. "I sent for him to come so that I might pay him back the money he had advanced for three years. I offered him some jewels that belonged to my grandmother. He laughed at me when we were alone, and said I had ruined my career by singing in the opera and had broken my word to him by meeting Griffeth and caring for him. I offered him the rubies—"

Dmitri bent over her suddenly.

"Rubies?" he repeated quickly. "What were they?"

"They belonged to Margherita Paoli, my grandmother. He had seen me wear them at the fête, and told me on the way home he wanted to buy them. But when I offered them to him, he—he refused. We were alone and I tried to fight him off. The lamp crashed to the floor and I felt his arms close about me; then I fainted."

Dmitri watched the long green curtains at the bedroom door. They were motionless, yet he crossed over and parted them casually to glance within.

"So," he said in relief. "And then? Do not hurry."

"I was unconscious for a while, and when I recovered the room was still in darkness. I found the push-button in the wall and turned on the lights. Mr. Ward lay on the floor by the couch. He made a sound of moaning and it frightened me. Oh, Dmitri, it was horrible to be alone with him there. I gave him water to drink and saw that he was wounded in the back. He told me to go quietly down and tell Ishigaki who was waiting for him in his car. I must be very careful and give no alarm, he said. He had been stabbed and the jewels were gone. After I had sent the Japanese up to help him, I was afraid to go myself. I wanted Griffeth. I knew they would try to keep me from him."

"Why did you not call him at the house on the Square?"

"I did," she protested. "He had not come in yet, they told me. I left word for him that I must see him."

Dmitri gazed at her glowing, expressive face with half-closed, retrospective eyes. Surely Fate had sent her to his door at the one hour of opportunity. He would save the boy Steccho from folly and crime, and give Griffeth back his love.

"Then he must have received your message after he left here," he said cheerily. "And he will surely seek you at your own home. You must go back there."

"I never will go back to them. I will wait for him here," she insisted. "They will blame me for everything, for sending to Mr. Ward, for the loss of the jewels, everything, and I will not listen to them. I do not care for anything in the whole world but Griffeth."

"Then you must safeguard him," Dmitri urged. "They may suspect him since he knew of the jewels, and we who live and think as nomads are ever under suspicion. Have you not heard it said that all genius is insanity? It is enough that he lives in the temperamental zone of the village. Now, my dear child, you are cold and nervous. You will see how well I can take care of you. You shall sit here and drink coffee for a few moments while I go and telephone to Griffeth. And then"—he knelt before the brazier, stirring and blowing the embers to a blaze—"then we will have the surprise. When you were very little, did you not always love the surprise, eh? Sometimes Life is still indulgent to us; even in our greatest extremity, she grants us the surprise, and it is this that keeps up our faith, that somehow, somewhere, our own shall come to us, see?"

"If he is there when you call up, will you tell him to come here to me?" She looked at him with longing eyes, and Dmitri smiled back at her.

"Surely I will. Fate shuffles the cards, remember; man only deals them. I have ever found that we move in circles of coincidence drawn together like the particles in the spectrum by some immutable unseen force of attraction to form a cosmic harmony. You like that, do you? For, see, you go forth in the night to seek your well-beloved, like the Shulamite of old. Do you know her, my dear, among the immortal lovers?" He measured level spoonfuls of pulverized coffee into the little copper pot carefully. "Yet you remind me of her. So. When this boils up the third time, then you shall drink it while I go for your surprise."

Out in the street a car drew up before the house next door. Count Jurka alighted, scanned the small brass numbers on the door carefully, and ascended the narrow steps. He wore a cloak over his evening suit, the cape thrown back over one shoulder, and as he waited he hummed a waltz air from the last opera he had heard in Bucharest. Surely the road of fortune lay free to the intrepid traveler. They had thought, with the sop of peace thrown to her, that Bulgaria would lie still like a whipped cur. The royalist cause was denied recognition save as the latest king licked the hand that fed him. Only in the old queen, rebellious and restless in her exile, was the spirit of dominion. He smiled as he recalled her favors.

"A straight line—a goal!"

The line from Nietzsche swam through his head. He felt supremely satisfied with life. The message from Steccho had reached him at the hotel and he had come himself. As he was directed by the sleepy houseman to the room at the top of the first flight of stairs, he balanced the boy's destiny for him. Was it wiser to silence him now or on the voyage back? He would leave it to Georges. Yet not even to him would he give the pleasure of receiving the royal rubies. He lit a cigarette at the head of the stairs and tapped on the door.

There was dead silence within. He tried the knob, and found the key turned on the inner side.

"Open," he said curtly. "It is I."

Steccho obeyed slowly. He had been sitting on the narrow cot, his head buried in his hands. His shirt was open at the throat as if it had choked him. In the dim light from the one gas-jet his face looked haggard and yellow under his long, straight, disheveled hair.

"You have kept me waiting." Jurka closed the door behind him, standing with his back to it. "Where are the jewels?"

The blood rushed to Steccho's head. He threw back his hair with a quick movement of his head, and smiled in the old servile way.

"I have them all, excellenza. One moment only. You can swear to me by your own life that I shall find all well at Rigl, that they will be there to greet me, my mother and little Maryna?"

Around the lips of the Count there curved an amused smile.

"I swear to you I will send you where they are," he said slowly.

As the meaning of his words flashed upon the boy, he flung himself forward, his fingers seizing his throat.

"Go thou before me!" he gasped. "Liar and murderer, see who it is that kills you! Look deep in my eyes! I, Ferad Steccho, send you out of life! Think on my mother!" His fingers choked the thin, white neck of Jurka relentlessly, but the Count fought back with all the advantage of a trained body and mind. They fell on the couch together, locked in a death-grapple. Almost without sound, save for the stifled breathing, they fought until Jurka wrenched himself free, and staggered back.

"Excellenza!" Steccho breathed, his face the very mask of hate, "I have heard the truth. They are dead these five months, my mother cut down by famine, my sister—Oh, God, hear me!—Maryna is dead, a woman thing thrown to your soldiers to be done to death at their pleasure; you hear me! You swore to me by the cross you would protect them, and you knew this all the time you lied to me. You knew when you sent me last night to rob and kill for you."

"If I call for help, what then?" sneered Jurka. "I will swear you robbed me."

"Call! Call on your queen to save you." The boy leaped upon him like a panther and bore him to the floor, his bare hands gripping remorselessly at the white, slim throat. He bent over the mottled, horror-stricken face, forcing the glazing eyes to stare into his, and laughed softly. "See, I could kill you with the knife, but I will have you look at me, so, straight to the door of death. Excellenza, the rubies are red. Think on the blood of the innocents you have killed, thousands and thousands. They wait for you—"

He felt the figure beneath him twist and strain with one last tremendous effort to force him off. The Count's hands fumbled blindly, searchingly, and there came a dull report. Hardly had Steccho felt the touch of the automatic as it was pressed to his side. The pain was deadened by the joy of watching the light die out of the staring, maddened eyes. His fingers loosened their grasp unwittingly. The form of Jurka crumpled to the floor, and Steccho pressed his hands against his side, looking at them curiously. Sinking into the chair by the low table, he pulled the jewels from his pockets. They were moist and dulled. What was it Dmitri had warned him?

"They are accursed. Red for the blood of your people, pearls for the tears they have shed."

He picked up the heavy tiara and dashed it down into the dead face upon the floor.

"Excellenza," he whispered, "think on them, they wait for you—" His head fell forward on his breast. The lines of the wall-paper seemed to dance and entwine as life slipped from his reach. "The sun shines on the yellow castle," he murmured huskily. "Maryna's hair, yellow in the sun, yellow like gold, excellenza, and wet with blood." He sighed heavily, groping for something with the seeking touch of the blind, something he had let fall when he had seized the white throat of Jurka. And suddenly there was utter silence in the room, the curious silence where there is no breath of life stirring.

Next door Dmitri paused on the steps as he closed the door behind him. In the east a glow of deepest rose flushed the mother-of-pearl clouds into shells of trembling, lambient radiance. He eyed it happily. It was a symbol, that promise of the daybreak. So in the earth-lands overseas the dawn of humanity was coming despite the upheavals of class struggles. He would come back and pack after he had returned Carlota safely to Griffeth, together with the jewels. Then he and Steccho would take the homeward way together. He glanced down the shadowy street. There was no one in sight. He entered the house by the basement door. The houseman smiled and nodded to him as he set out empty milk bottles. He mounted the stairs with a light, buoyant step and knocked at Steccho's door. There was no response, and he pushed the door open. Something there was inside that lay close against it, impeding his entrance, and he peered around, thinking the boy had slept there in heavy exhaustion.

"Ferad!" he called cheerily. "It is daybreak. You sleep late."

But the boy did not stir. He slept well in the last bivouac, and, turning, Dmitri beheld the other stark form beside him, he who had been the court chamberlain, the debonair Jurka, the queen's messenger. Crushed in the hand of Steccho was the letter from Sofia. He unclenched the stiffened fingers gently and read it with half-closed eyes and contracted muscles. Placing it in his own inner pocket, he searched both bodies. On Jurka he found a leather wallet filled with bank-notes and documents. There was no time to examine them. He noticed only the Count's personal card and the address, the Hotel Dupont. In another pocket was a bunch of keys which he took. Not a sign was there in the room of the jewels. Only in Steccho's raincoat pocket he discovered a large unset opal, one of those toys Ward had played with, kept by the boy to please Maryna. He went out as he had come, nodding again to the houseman.

There was no time to waste. There would be the hue and cry of the police and newspapers. He would be brought into it inevitably. Outside the house he paused and lighted a cigarette deliberately, then sauntered to the corner where a light burned all night in the little Bulgarian café of Barouki. It was part of the creed of life to Barouki not to ask questions of any one, which attribute rendered his place popular among those who came from Sofia. Dmitri greeted the sleepy-eyed old man, and entered the dusty booth at the end of the café. His voice was pleasant and comradely as he called the apartment of Ogden Ward.

"But you will be kind enough to disturb him, nevertheless," he urged upon Ishigaki. "Tell him I have an opal to return to him."

Dmitri came from the café with a little smile on his lips. He hailed a becalmed taxi in front of a chop-house near the elevated station, and drove back for Carlota.

"I should never have come to you, should I?" she asked, tiredly, as she leaned her head back on the cushions. "What was the surprise?"

"My very dear child," he said tenderly, "you must trust me. I believe in fate and opportunity, in what we call in my land the hour appointed, and never in my life have I been permitted to watch the gods at work so much as now. Sleep awhile as we drive uptown. I will waken you at Fifty-Ninth Street, where I leave you. And you must not be afraid. Love is eternal. Nothing can kill it. Remember that. Only keep faith with yourself."

He watched her lips relax and her lashes droop. As the car hurried uptown through silent streets the hum of the city gradually began, the far-off call of the ferry-boats sounded in the gray sea mist, a fire engine clanged down Fourth Avenue. Dmitri folded his arms, looking straight ahead of him, and seeing two set faces under the flickering gaslight. They had passed out of the play, Jurka and the boy Ferad. Who had profited by their death? The queen's rubies still lured with their unholy splendor another's feet along the trail of death.

CHAPTER XIX

THE telephone bell rang in the living-room. Carlota lifted her head eagerly from the pillow to listen as Maria answered.

"It is quite impossible. Miss Trelango is ill and cannot come to the telephone herself."

"Oh, Maria, but I can—please—" Carlota called breathlessly from the inner bedroom, but the voice went on inexorably and with chill finality.

"I regret I cannot listen any further. It is impossible for her to see you."

Carlota sat up in bed, slim and tragic, her wealth of dark hair tumbling about her shoulders.

"Was that Mr. Ames? You begged me to come and talk to Jacobelli not five minutes ago, and now you say that I am too ill to get up."

"Cara mia, you are not to excite yourself with anger," Maria soothed her. "Lie very still, my preciosa, relax your nerves. Remember agitation is very bad for your voice."

"But you will not understand, Maria," she protested. "This is the man I love, the man I shall surely marry, and you will not even let me speak to him when I know how troubled he is. I must see him, Maria. If you really loved me, you would not keep us apart."

"Would I not?" Maria repeated fervently. "How did he know this number?"

"I do not know," Carlota asserted proudly. "I did not even tell him my name, nothing at all."

"So? Then it is maybe—the Marchese. He is soft-hearted. He regards this as a romance when it is a calamity. Do you realize what it means, Jacobelli saying Ward insists everything is to be canceled if you persist in jeopardizing your career?"

"Mr. Ward?" Carlota smiled. "When did he say that? Not today surely?"

"You are concealing something from me." Maria bent over her with wide, accusing eyes, even while her fingers stroked her hair fondly. "Ah, if I had never gone to Casanova's reception, I might have saved you everything, the wild escapade at this Mrs. Nevins's, the exposé, the loss of the jewels, the horror of last night—Now, behold, your career is ruined."

Carlota was silent, her eyes bright with anger. It was all they thought of, the money which Ward had given for her musical education, the door which he might have opened for her to success. They thought that life was made up only of achievement. Even Maria, whom she had loved and leaned upon always, had veered completely over to the enemy, and found a sacred obligation in keeping her thus, behind the wall of Tittani. She closed her eyes as Maria's voice declaimed solemnly:

"With the world at her feet, Paoli tossed it aside like a withered flower and retired to her villa with only her friends and her memories. Bianca, your beloved mother, fled with her love and died, still half a child. This is only the very first false dawn of love, carina. You will forget him in a month. Ah, if I could but take you back, for even a little while, to the garden."

"If you try to part us, I will never sing again," Carlota told her tragically. "I will never accept any aid from Mr. Ward again."

"Then you are what Jacobelli called you, an ingrate, after all the love and hope we have lavished upon you." Maria was weeping plenteously, helplessly, as she realized the power behind Carlota's words.

The outer bell rang, silencing the argument. Hurriedly she went to open it, while the girl slipped from the bed, flung a silk robe over her shoulders, and slipped her feet into satin mules. If it should be Griffeth, if he had really dared to come again to penetrate her tower of durance, she would force them to let her see him. She listened eagerly for his voice. Instead it was a messenger boy, bearing Ames's first shell into the enemy's camp. He had gone from the telephone booth, and had spent all he had in an orgy of roses from a flower-stand.

"Return them. There is no answer," Maria said firmly.

But the boy was loyal. Stolidly he insisted there was no place to return them. The gentleman had gone on his way. In the doorway Carlota appeared suddenly and Maria stepped back from the look in her eyes as she took the long box as if it had been a tiny bambino. Holding it close to her breast, she went back to her bed, her chin pressed against it.

"I shall not even speak to you or look at you, if you treat me like this, Maria. I am not a child," she said haughtily. "Whatever he sends to me, you will regard it as sacred."

"You are not responsible. You are unreasonable and reckless, and I shall lock you in your room. The Marchese and Jacobelli will be here later, and then you will tell them the truth about last night."

"I will tell them nothing." Carlota held her breath, listening to the turn of the lock in the door, and shrugged her shoulders as she laid her face on the red roses. It would not do to break her heart in solitude, not when she knew he was thinking of her and trying to reach her. Dmitri would surely find him and tell him all that had occurred the previous night. He would clear him of any charge Ward might lodge against him. What charge could they bring, save that he had befriended the boy Steccho and had loved her? Ingrate, they called her. The word puzzled her. She found her little red morocco dictionary in her desk drawer and looked it up in deepest interest. The definition was brief and to the point:

"Ingrate: One who is ungrateful."

Sitting up in bed, girl fashion, she leaned her elbows on her knees, and thought seriously. The melody of *Cerca d'Amore* ran through her mind, the quest of love, and all her being seemed to become, in some mystical sense, a chalice to hold this divine essence of love that had glorified her life. Impulsively she turned the pages to the word "love." The definition was vague and unsatisfactory.

"Love: to have affection."

She pursed her lips, and gravely sought another route to knowledge.

"Husband: a man who marries a woman."

This was utterly absurd to a seeker after life's greatest, sweetest mystery. She hurried to "wife," and found merely an echo.

"Wife: a woman who marries a man."

Last of all, she found "marriage." It was positively trite.

"Marriage: wedlock."

Under "wedlock" she discovered "marriage." She hurled the little book from her, and seized a pencil and pad from the stand beside her.

"Love," she dashed off impetuously, "the divine gift that joins two hearts for eternity."

This looked nearer the ecstasy of real truth. Not that one could even approach in words the expression of the miracle of love, but this was closer. In the next room Maria sang a tender old chant of the nuns at Leguna Marino, the tiny town that clung to the cliffs below Villa Tittani. This was a ruse, to lift her mind from earthly things, she knew, and yet she tried again, her own improvements in the lexicon of love.

"Marriage," she wrote carefully. "The blessed union of two souls who love perfectly."

It was an inspired improvement on the dictionary definition, she thought, and after "love" she added, "the divine gift that awakens souls to life's meaning."

Maria would never understand. She would smile at her pityingly and guard her from the passion that was her heritage. Jacobelli would rage and beat the air and denounce all romance as a detractor of art, but the old Marchese, he would sympathize with her. Sometimes, when he sat at dinner with them, smoking leisurely, a smile of content on his fine old face, she had often wondered what memories lay behind his charm of manner and unfailing understanding with youth's heritage of yearning. With the rose on the pillow beside her and the little pad in her hand, she fell asleep.

In the living-room Maria Roma knelt beside the Florentine chest, selecting the remainder of the Paoli collection to be deposited in the safety vault. It was true, as Ward had told Jacobelli the previous night, coming from the Nevins fête, neither Carlota nor she had appreciated the full value of the royal gems. The stolen rubies alone were worth several hundred thousand dollars, yet Carlota had worn them as if they had been paste. There was not another stone in the world that could compare in purity with the Zarathustra ruby. Maria knew the story of how it had come into the possession of Margherita Paoli, nearly half a century before. She had heard of the impassioned young Balkan prince who had cast all he owned at the feet of the most beautiful woman in Europe. When she would have returned the rubies, he had refused them, even with the knowledge of her affair with Tennant.

"You deny me your love. Let the rubies tell you ever of mine. I may not hold you in my arms. Let them rest on your glorious hair, your throat, your breast, telling you forever that Boris loved you."

Yet it was doubtful whether Paoli herself had even grasped the great value of the jewels. She had never been the type of woman to seek the price of anything. It belittled rather than enhanced the value of a thing to have it rated. So the rubies had lain for years in the old chest with her other jewels, half forgotten as the years went by, and Crown Prince Boris had long since lain upon his gold and purple catafalque.

Delicately and precisely Maria placed each remaining piece in its separate velvet case, sighing heavily over her task. The burden of responsibility laid by the old Contessa upon her shoulders, weighed heavily in the present crisis. Love or ambition? Which pathway was the feet of girlhood to follow when genius had given wings for flight? It would be fatal for Carlota, on the threshold of her career, to marry as her mother had done, flinging all into the balance of romance. Yet there came a thrill to Maria's Trentino blood as she realized how the old Marchese sympathized with such recklessness.

It was all quite simple, he had told her the previous night when they had returned and found Carlota gone, the jewels stolen, and Ishigaki caring for Ward. While Ward had smiled at her inscrutably as she wept and demanded the truth, the old Marchese had ignored him, and had calmed her gently.

"Whatever has happened, there is no cause for alarm. Youth and art, a boy and girl singing love duets together, pouf! What would they have come from such a tragedy, she and Jacobelli, and Mr. Ward himself? Compel a girl like Carlota to don gray and walk softly to set measures like some little novice, a girl with the Trelango and Paoli blood beating love's tempo in her veins!"

"But her voice, her career?" she had protested wildly. "Is it nothing, all we have done and hoped for her?"

The Marchese had smiled tenderly.

"Jacobelli is a great teacher," he said, "but there is one greater than he. His heartstrings are insulated copper wires, my dear Maria. And for the rubies—remember what the old Contessa herself used to say of them, that they were accursed, pearls for the tears of an oppressed people, rubies for the blood of the innocent? Regret them not. I have never craved such things myself, not while there is truth and beauty and love left to us to cherish."

Carlota slept heavily, dreamlessly, the sleep of utter exhaustion of mind and body after the long night. Through her windows the late autumn sunlight poured an amber glow. A mellow stillness seemed to lie over the city as if the hush of Indian summer had already laid a finger upon the laughing lips of Manhattan. Even the ringing of the outer bell when the Marchese arrived failed to rouse her. He was smiling and debonair as ever, bearing his customary votive offering of flowers. Laying his gloves upon his hat on the piano, he beamed upon Maria's anxious face.

"Cheer up, my friend," he exclaimed. "The world is very beautiful this afternoon. Where is Carlota? So, asleep." He lowered his voice. "That is better, for you and I, Maria, have seen life, have looked it in the face and not quailed, have we not, and we are not afraid, where she is very young and tender."

"Ah, what now?" Maria whispered, her hands pressed to her temples. "He is not here?"

"He? Who, the boy Griffeth? No, no, my dear, he is not here. In fact, he may be quite safe behind prison bars by night. That would please you, yes?"

"In prison? For persecuting her with his attentions?"

"No, for complicity in the attempt to murder Ogden Ward and the robbery of the jewels. I have just come from Ward himself. He is not injured seriously. The ribs deflected the blow. His greatest wish is to avoid all publicity—naturally."

The sardonic note in his tone struck Maria.

"You surely do not place any reliance in what she said last night? She was excited and distraught. A child like that would mistake the fervor of love for an attack—"

She stopped short. Carlota stood in the doorway, slim and erect in a hasty toilette. She had overheard their voices and arisen. With the long refreshing sleep had come high resolve. The Marchese, looking at her arrayed in a long, clinging négligé of creamy lace, with its borders of rich fur, thought of the young Paoli in her first fire of love.

"Ah, cara mia," exclaimed Maria eagerly, "you have rested. Kiss your old cross Maria, so. We dine with the Marchese tonight; you will like that, yes?"

Carlota shook her head, her eyes brilliant with resentment and determination.

"I will not go," she said passionately. "You have treated me as if I were a spoiled child, locking me in my room. What is this about Ward accusing Griffeth, Marchese? He was not even here last night."

"But where was he, then, my child? The night doorman tells another story. He was here after you had left."

Carlota's eyes closed and opened again widely, fearlessly.

"Mr. Ward dares to accuse Griffeth of the robbery and attack on himself, does he?"

"No. He is very considerate, my dear, very kind," Veracci assured her tenderly. "You are over-anxious and must not lose the perspective of things. Mr. Ward has silenced the news of the robbery. There is nothing at all in the papers. He is handling the entire affair most diplomatically, with private detectives, and the police commissioner muzzled. Ah, he is very clever. His own wound is nothing to him, but the loss of the jewels is everything. His theory is this, you have been meeting friends of Ames, no doubt, in his studio. You may have spoken of the jewels—"

"I did not!" flashed Carlota.

"Possibly without intent. You wore them at the fête. There has been a secret search going on for these royal gems, it appears, for months. Ward knew all about it. He did not know they were in your possession until the night of the fête, he says. They are part of the crown jewels of Bulgaria."

"But they were given to Margherita outright by Boris himself," protested Maria; "there was no theft. They were hers."

"He had no right to give them." The old Marchese spoke gently. "When the revolution came and Ferdinand fled, Sophia took the crown jewels with her. Since then, Ward tells me, parts of them have been turning up at every jewel mart in the world, where she has sought to raise funds for the royalist cause. These were traced to America from Italy by a man named Count Jurka, the queen's chamberlain. Ward knew him. He was found dead this morning."

Maria stared at him in silence. Carlota came to his side quickly, her face white with dread, as she remembered Dmitri's promise to find the jewels.

"Where?"

"In a room on East Twenty-Eighth Street. It is in the Bulgarian quarter, next door to where a man lives named Dmitri Kavec, the closest friend of Griffeth Ames. My dear," as his arm encircled her swaying figure, "you must be strong. He was found with another, a Bulgarian boy called Steccho, also a friend of Ames and Kavec's. Have you met them at his studio?"

"I know Dmitri Kavec," she said brokenly, her hands covering her face. "Has he accused Griffeth?"

"He has not been found himself. That is why they are going to hold the boy as witness against him, and for possible complicity in the crime. Did you see the man who entered this room last night and took the jewels?"

Carlota stared up at him almost beseechingly, and shook her head.

"I fainted when Mr. Ward's arms touched me." She shuddered at the memory of that moment. "But I know Dmitri is not guilty." She hesitated. Dmitri, Griffeth's friend, to whom she had gone last night in her trouble. His buoyant words rang in her mind when he had left her. She was to have no fear. He would recover the jewels for her and bring them to her. Did he have them in his possession at that very moment? Was it all part of some secret conspiracy to escape with them himself, defrauding not only her, but Jurka as well? She lifted her head with swift resolution.

"I am going to Griffeth. No, you cannot hold me, Maria. Come with me if you like, but I am going to him. He will need me greatly. If you will not, then I must ask the Marchese to take me to him."

And Maria Roma, looking into her eyes, knew the days of girlhood had passed and the feet of Paoli's grandchild had scaled the wall of Tittani in her quest for love.

CHAPTER XX

Sauntering from the elevated station at Eighth Street over to the Square, Jacobelli mused upon the vagaries of a golden voice. His point of view was changing with the speed of an Alpine tourist. Maria had acquainted him with the decision of Carlota.

"Ah, signor, believe me, she does not feign illness. Her heart is not breaking. It is freezing, which is worse. Never will she sing again, she declares, if you deny her the one whom she loves. She spoke his name in her sleep. It is the romance beautiful, the divine fire from heaven alighted upon the altar of a woman's heart, it is—"

"Enough!" exclaimed Jacobelli. "I capitulate. Doubtless she is right. Two—three years nearly I have taught her all I know, and yet what is it? She cannot sing the wonderful heart-throb music as the great woman artiste must. Not all the technique in the world can put it into her voice; yet one day she meets the man she loves, and lo! it is there, she excels. I knew it when she came to me that day at the studio after she had quarreled with him. I heard it then in her voice, the glory—the abandon—the power of the woman who claims the universe for her love. And I am a fool, Maria, I lose my head entirely. I am jealous of this unknown teacher who has opened the heart of my star. I hate him. At the Nevins fête I make the grand fool of myself, signora. But now, I see, I bow. Let her have her love if she will. I have lunched with the Marchese, and am at peace with the world. After the honeymoon tell her we will resume her lessons."

He felt marvelously benevolent as he made his way towards Ames's studio. Possibly his luncheon chat with the Marchese had much to do with it, also the fact that later he had seen Casanova. Count D'Istria had kept his word to Griffeth, and Casanova, ever ready to observe the way of the wind with managerial straws, had promised to bring the operetta to the immediate attention of the Metropolitan directors with his sanction on its production the coming season.

Finding his way up the three flights of stairs, Jacobelli knocked upon the door with his cane. Griffeth lay full length upon the cushions of the dormer window-seat, depressed and miserable. He had been awake all night, striving to get into communication with Carlota or Dmitri, and had missed them at every point. Still his flowers had not been returned. He had ascertained that much from the lad at the flower-stand in the old market. He had sent twice to Dmitri's house and he had not returned since daybreak, they said.

The rap on the outer door made him spring to unlock it, expecting either Dmitri or a message from Carlota. Instead there stood upon his threshold Guido Jacobelli, from whom he had been parted by interested friends only a night before, the one man in New York whom he regarded as his enemy. He gave him no invitation to enter, but stood like a glowering, expectant young stag, ready for the onslaught of his adversary.

Jacobelli waved him aside airily, and entered the room, making himself at home in the large oak armchair, and stroking Ptolemy who strolled over to inspect him.

"We make friends, what you say, my boy?" he asked genially. "I forgive you from my heart all you do to me in the past, see? Why? Because I, Jacobelli, make the great discovery. You speak the truth. She is your pupil."

"What do you mean?" asked Griffeth suspiciously. "I heard all that you said of her last evening. I understand perfectly that she is Paoli's granddaughter and backed by the patronage of Ogden Ward. I do not know why it was her whim to come down here and play at being my pupil. It has ruined my work and broken my heart, but I wish her all the success and happiness in the world."

Jacobelli beamed at him archly, his black eyebrows rising in crescents, his lips a smiling, close curve above his two double chins.

"She came here because she loves you, my boy, because she longed to give you her wonderful voice in your operetta. She is Love's pupil. One day she opens her mouth to sing for me, and, my God! It is there, the temperament I have prayed for, it is there, and you have given it to her. I salute you."

"Has she sent you to me?" asked Griffeth eagerly. "May I see her at once?"

Jacobelli chuckled, stroking the yellow fur of Ptolemy until it crackled.

"I know nothing of her. I have not seen her since last night, but the Signora Roma tells me she has tormented them all because they would not permit her to see you. In fact, she tried to reach you last night; you knew this?"

"I found her message when I returned. I tried to see her and walked back home through the Park."

"Which is just as well." The old maestro smiled significantly. "Youth is utterly mad. You rave now, and say your career is ended. My poor boy, you have not heard from Casanova, no? This very hour he tells me they will surely produce your operetta next season. Is not that enough?"

"The operetta?" repeated Griffeth grimly. "I had forgotten all about it. When I lost her everything went out of my life. I felt like using the world for a football and kicking the stars up a little higher out of reach. You don't know how blank life seemed to me until she came down here. I had been across during the war with Carrollton Phelps in the Aerial Service. We fell about the same time, and after months of being patched up, I was sent home, excess baggage on the war wagon. I was twenty then, and when I had my grip back, my father let me do as I pleased, and I came here to work out some of the things I had always hoped to do. I've felt like an idler beating out harmonies in this bird's-eye castle until she came."

"Then I will tell you something to comfort you and light the path again. Always remember the path is there even though you are in darkness." Jacobelli pressed his finger-tips together, his eyes brilliant with the fire of enthusiasm. "One of your own great men has said he would rather write the songs of a nation than its laws. We are but teachers, my boy. You who compose music are the living current between humanity and those mighty, immutable laws of harmony and vibration which move the universe, is it not so?—and love is the greatest of all divine laws."

From a street piano at the curb below the studio windows the melody of the *Barcarole* came to them in ascending volume. A taxicab drew up beside it. Carlota could almost have blown kisses to each dear, remembered spot along the Square as she alighted with Maria. Only forty-eight hours since she had been to the studio, yet the tidal wave of circumstance had nearly swept the happiness of her life out to sea. She smiled at the Greek boy beside the pushcart, smiled at the children playing in the patches of ground before the old brownstone row of houses, smiled almost in the face of Sergeant Lorrie, of the Central Detective Bureau, as she passed him on the steps.

Maria followed her, resigned and tragic. She had called up the Marchese at the final moment, even after he had left them and returned to the Lafayette, to tell him Carlota's ultimate choice, and to her amazement the old Italian courtier had congratulated her on her own defeat.

"Remember, signora," he had urged buoyantly, a "certain ancient gentleman of varied experience in matrimony, one King Solomon, has stated as his opinion that love is stronger than death and many waters cannot quench it. I agree with him perfectly. Request our beloved Carlota that she will permit my presence at her nuptials with Pierrot. I have a penchant for romantic weddings. They recall to me the fragrance of roses abloom at Vallombrosa. Once, as we two walked under the olive grove years ago, you refused me, Maria mia. When you are tempted to be unyielding and forbidding to these children, these two lovers, remember Vallombrosa, I implore you. Had you said yes, I should not have carried the fragrance of roses as a bitter-sweet memory all my life long."

So it happened that, despite her sense of duty to the last wishes of the old Contessa, Maria felt a thrill of sympathy in the great adventure as she followed Carlota into the studio on the top floor.

"We have come for Carlota's sake," she said majestically. "It is against my wishes and judgment, but we are here, signor. You have won."

"What is it, dear?" exclaimed Griffeth, as he held Carlota's hands in his. "You are cold as ice, and trembling." He drew her favorite Roman chair forward to the open grate fire, but Carlota drew back.

There were shadows beneath her eyes and entreaty in the glance she gave him.

"Have you heard from Dmitri?"

"Not a word since midnight. I left him then; why?"

She sank into the chair as he stooped eagerly to rouse the fire to a blaze. "Why, it is almost laughable to find you here just as always, perfectly safe, and you even seem happy."

"I am happy. Jacobelli has just left me and we are great friends. He came to tell me the operetta is accepted by Casanova. Isn't that great news, dear?"

"And you have heard nothing at all of what—what happened last night? No one has been here?"

"No one. What do you mean?" He rose as Maria crossed to the window and watched the Square below.

"The Marchese came and told us. Oh, Griffeth, it is all so horrible, and I know, I know that you had nothing to do with it. You do not need to tell me so."

He held her close in his arms as she reached out to him, and Maria told the news quickly, of the robbery and attack on Ward.

"They have implicated you because of your association with one of the men who is dead and the man who is missing, Dmitri."

"Dmitri!" repeated Griffeth. "What do you mean? Dmitri is my friend. Who is dead?"

"Griffeth, do you remember"—Carlota lifted her head from his shoulder—"the young Bulgarian I told you always followed me? The one Dmitri recognized from the window here and told me I was never to fear him? This morning we heard from the old Marchese that a double murder had been committed next door to where Dmitri lived. No, please do not speak yet," as he gave a startled exclamation. "One of the men was the Bulgarian boy, and they suspect Dmitri."

"And you yourself, because you are his friend," Maria added solemnly. "The Marchese assured us you would be arrested for complicity."

"But why did you come here last night?"

Carlota hesitated, but Maria's eyes were tender.

"Because I wanted you to help me," she said slowly. "There was no one else to go to, and I was in trouble. Mr. Ward came to the apartment to buy my rubies and while he was there he was assaulted and robbed."

"Were you hurt?"

"I fainted." Carlota's lashes drooped before his steady gaze. "And afterwards I was afraid to go back."

"Why?" he demanded.

Maria's hands fluttered out eagerly.

"You must not ask her disturbing questions when she is so nervous. It is all very terrible, and mostly so for me. I was to have protected and guarded her, and now, behold, it is as if she was utterly alone and friendless."

"Oh, do not even think about me!" Carlota cried passionately. "Where is Dmitri, Griffeth? You believe in him, do you not? Maria, leave me here alone. I must speak to him in confidence. Forgive me, tanta mia, I love and trust you, but this concerns his friend. You will go, just for a little while, won't you?"

The roses of Vallombrosa. Signora Roma met the pleading look in her eyes and the words of the old Marchese rang in her mind like a sacred charge. Romance and youth and Vallombrosa. If she had not been ambitious too, and had set her art ahead of love, what a long fair road of companionship and happiness life might have been with Bernardo Dinari, Marchese di Veracci. The tears rushed to her eyelids, and she sighed heavily in surrender as she folded Carlota to her breast.

"Take her from us," she said to Griffeth. "Ah, I am no longer blind and hard of heart. You have taught her well, signor, and after all, it is life's sweetest and richest song. I will go and walk in the Square and think I am back in Italy."

Ames closed the door behind her, leaning against it, looking longingly at the girl standing in the light from the dormer windows. Ptolemy leaped up to her, rubbing his tawny length affectionately against her, his eyes gleaming like topaz.

"Dear, look at me," he said eagerly. "You came to me again, just as you did that first day, my wonder girl. Even after everything, you had faith in me—"

She held her hands out to him, giving them to his clasp, yet holding him back.

"Have we any right to take our own happiness when it makes so many wretched? Maria, who brought me up and gave me all her love and care, and dear old Jacobelli—"

"But they are all willing now. It isn't selfish, dear. It is our right. Remember how Dmitri always said we were the inheritors of all the love dreams of the past, and must hold the torch high for those who come after us. You know all you have been to me for months, what it meant to both of us that first night at Phelps's when you met my eyes, and it seemed as if everything in my whole being called out to you in gladness. Carlota, don't keep me from you! Why did you come here last night to find me, why are you here today, why did Jacobelli come and tell me frankly it was our love that had given your voice its power and new beauty? Yet I've never even kissed you once, never held you in my arms—"

Her eyes closed as his arms clasped about her and he turned her towards him in a silent, tense embrace. When she lifted her head, she was smiling, her lashes wet with tears.

"This is not the right ending for the opera. I have passed the wall of Tittani and found you and there is no peril or suspense at all, just the two of us here in the dear old studio, and Ptolemy to turn his back and not look at us. He is a gentleman, isn't he, Griffeth?"

Across the Square along the diagonal path to the old studio building Dmitri walked with an easy, long-stepped gait. The troops that had surged over the Belachrista Pass had the same stride. The collar of his coat was turned up, his brown felt hat pulled low over his eyes, his cigarette pointing upward. He had passed a pleasant and profitable night. So engrossed he was in smiling at the future that he failed to observe Signora Roma waiting in the circle by the fountain, failed to notice three loiterers about the old studio row. One watched the dormer windows of the garret. One stood at the corner of MacDougal Street to take note of possible exits over adjacent roofs in case of need. One leaned against the iron railing in the front yard and chatted with the unwitting caretaker, and Dmitri passed them all by jauntily. Would it be wiser, he mused, to tell Griffeth Ames everything? He had trained him for months in the new law of humanity's rights, yet was he not too young to recognize the imperative need for silence. The breaking dawn called to Dmitri's imagination. The chant of the oppressed sounded in his ears, not the old galley chorus that had kept time to the rhythm of an Attic boatswain's flute, nor the call from the steppe prisons that had been the newborn wail of Russia's freedom. The old order had already changed. The heavens were rolling away as a parchment before the new dayspring. A little struggling here and there, he told himself, over the earth's surface, a little blindness in the new light from eyes long used to darkness, but steadily, inevitably the daybreak would sweep on and in the full sunlight men should find themselves gazing into one another's eyes without fear and hatred and greed.

He mounted the three flights rapidly, two steps at a time, tapped on the door, and opened before Griffeth could reach it.

"Aha!" cried Dmitri. "And so we may be sure that spring will come again! Are you Harlequin or Pierrot this afternoon, or all the immortal lovers of romance at once? And have you coffee for a wayfarer? I have walked all over the city since daybreak. I see that in spite of my precautions, Columbine has found her way right straight back to the chimney-pot and the cat and the melody of one Pierrot."

He sank down in the old dusty velvet chair by the fireplace, his hair tousled into curls. Carlota gazed at him with wondering, questioning eyes. Dmitri, no subtle, terrified criminal hiding from the law, but as she had ever known him, the happy, confident, scholarly friend. She forgot everything but his danger.

"Why"—she turned appealingly to Griffeth—"it's almost laughable—it's like some horrible dream—that I am here with you both just as always, and you are safe, Dmitri—"

"Why should I not be safe?" He smiled at her with keen, brilliant eyes. "It is a most charming surprise to find you here, I admit. I was only going to drop in and see my favorite friend before I leave. I was going to entrust to him a commission, but since you are here—"

The door of the studio opened noiselessly. Dmitri's lips were silenced by the sight behind Griffeth and the girl. Lorrie, of the Central Bureau, was not a person of dramatic instincts or emotional possibilities. He stood in the patch of sunlight from the hall skylight, his hands in his pockets, his hat pushed back on his head. The hands grasped two automatics, but Lorrie never obtruded them on the sensibilities of those he was sent to find until he found it necessary. He stepped into the room, a slight smile on his lips as he took in the group. Behind him stood two of his men.

"Kavec," he said curtly, "you're under arrest for the double murder of Jurka and Steccho."

Dmitri never stirred.

"But he is my friend, Carrollton Phelps's friend!" exclaimed Griffeth hotly. "I was with him up to midnight myself."

"Don't worry, you're in too," returned Lorrie laconically. "Complicity in the robbery, accessory to the crime, and then some. Search them."

"But I was with Mr. Kavec myself until early this morning," Carlota declared suddenly, her face lifted high, her eyes avoiding Griffeth's. "He had nothing to do with the robbery. He did not even know about it until I told him myself. It is impossible that he could have done this thing—"

She stopped dead short, the color leaving her lips. From Dmitri's pockets the detectives drew the rubies of the exiled queen. One by one the separate pieces were laid upon the table, the necklace, the loosely linked pendants, the girdle ornament.

Dmitri lit a cigarette with steady fingers.

"The tiara is inside my other coat," he said. "It would be a shame to break the set."

"Dmitri, my God, what have you done!" gasped Griffeth. "Carlota, go to Maria, out of this. I swear I knew absolutely nothing. Dmitri, tell her Steccho gave them to you, didn't he? Say something, man, can't you?"

"He's got nothing to say," Lorrie answered. "Look here." He threw out papers on the table from Dmitri's coat pockets. "Passage engaged for Naples, sailing tomorrow. A quick get-away, eh, Kavec."

"I do not believe one word of it!" flashed Carlota. "Who ordered this arrest? The jewels were mine. I have made no complaint of being robbed. Oh, I do not want any of them back. I hate the sight of them."

She sank down in a chair, her face covered by her hands, her shoulders shaken with sobs, deep, tearless, broken sobs of hopelessness. As Ogden Ward entered the room hers was the first form his eyes rested on. Leaning heavily upon a cane and Ishigaki's arm, he walked slowly, and with evident pain. Behind him was the tall, dignified figure of the Marchese, his kindly face troubled and keen when he beheld the group within the studio.

"My dear child"—he was beside Carlota instantly. "I am so very sorry for you. I never dreamt of all this. I deemed it my duty to acquaint Mr. Ward with your intention to come here as proof of your finality, and he would come also, therefore I am with him."

Dmitri's gaze never left the face of Ward. Steadily he looked at him, not sardonically nor with any animosity, but rather whimsically and pityingly.

"You brought this on yourself, Ames," Ward said slowly. "I did it to protect the interests of Miss Trelango. Through the criminal associates she met in your place here, she lost hundreds of thousands of dollars worth in jewels. I resolved, after hearing her decision from the Marchese, to tell her myself of your deliberate sacrifice of her to get possession of these gems. From the first moment that I learned of the double murder, I myself took up the pursuit of the guilty parties with the commissioner himself, and this is the result."

"Pardon." Ward started at the first sound of Dmitri's voice, suave and evenly pitched, as if he had heard it before. "When was that first moment, if one may ask, Mr. Ward?"

Ward's face set in deeper lines. Only Dmitri and he himself of all those in the room knew the menace behind the words. Until that instant he had not known of the presence there of one who had spoken to him over the wire at daybreak that morning. Lorrie looked at the banker sharply, waiting for his reply.

"You don't have to be annoyed by him, you know, Mr. Ward. My orders are to bring them both down to headquarters."

Ward lifted his hand.

"I will be responsible, sergeant," he said coldly. "Wait below."

With the Marchese's arm around her, Carlota watched in amazement the man she loved, the man who hated him, and Dmitri last of all. He was smiling, courteous as ever, thoroughly at ease and even enjoying the situation.

"May I draw your attention, Mr. Ward," he remarked, motioning to the table where the jewels lay. "See, they are there. I was bringing them here to give them to their rightful owner, Miss Trelango. It was best that she should not see me, so I was about to transfer them to the care of my friend, Mr. Ames. They are all there, not one missing. Stay. There is one the genial sergeant overlooked, but it is not of that set." He reached in his pocket and drew out his tobacco pouch. "For safe-keeping," he smiled, and produced the opal which Steccho had saved for the golden-haired Maryna to play with.

Ward's eyes stared at it fixedly, seeing instead the room at Carlota's apartment, the shattered lamp, the scattered gems, and one lithe, leaping figure in the dim oblong of light from the open window.

"I have seen that before," murmured the Marchese thoughtfully, "a beautiful gem."

"When I spoke to you on the telephone this morning I asked you if you had lost a jewel?" Dmitri's tone took on a keener edge as he leaned his hands upon the bare ebony table between them, and addressed Ward. "I also told you that I had just discovered a most unfortunate accident which had cost Count Jurka his life. I suggested, in view of certain papers which I had found in the Count's notebook regarding—"

"You are a criminal now in the eyes of the law," Ward cut in. "You know the value of a criminal's testimony."

"I am not speaking in court. I speak to my friends," said Dmitri gently. "And I am no criminal, save at your own good pleasure, Mr. Ward. Would you prefer that I state the facts here, or wait until we arrive at police headquarters or possibly the grand jury?"

Ward's face seemed to turn gray as they looked upon him.

"You can't prove a damned word." His eyes, bright and round, met Dmitri's in sudden challenge.

"Can I not?" laughed the latter cheerily. "Ah, my dear Mr. Ward, life is so very strange and so amusing, and so unexpected, and yet it is all one grand harmony. I show to you the jewels, the rubies and pearls of the royal collection. You know where I got them from, and yet you can sit there and threaten me. You are a fool, because I have the proof against you!"

Ward rose heavily.

"Call Lorrie," he gasped. "Marchese, I demand it."

"You will not call any one until you have heard me out," Dmitri said deliberately. "I have the signed confession and all the correspondence that passed between you and Georges Yaranek."

The Marchese moved away from Carlota to the table. She turned to Griffeth in relief, both of them listening in silent amazement to Dmitri's story.

"This man, Ogden Ward, is not the person he seems to be," he said almost gayly, yet with accusation. "He is not your silent, stern capitalist and banker, your international pawn-broker who can kill or

save a nation by his munificent charity. He is also of a most exquisite artistic temperament, a nature which responds to the richest and
priceless in art and beauty. He will have only the best, your Mr. Ward.
And this is known all over the world by those who live upon loot for
gold. It was not enough that Count Jurka should recover the missing
crown jewels. He must convert them into cash for use in the royalist
cause. And through his own researches he discovered another on the
same trail, the trail of the Zarathustra ruby. This was Ogden Ward,
who wished to add it to his collection, together with the Orient pearls
and other rubies of the set. Jurka had not been dispatched upon this
secret mission alone. Always, in such cases, there are two set forth
together, that one may succeed if one should fail. Steccho had told
me this, and of the court chamberlain's trusted attendant and courier,
Georges Yaranek. He is very clever, but he is nervous. When he discovered the two dead bodies he lost his nerve. And he left behind two
most important things, the wallet of Jurka, and this letter in the dead
hand of my friend."

From the inner hatband of his soft felt hat he removed the crumpled paper Steccho's hand had groped for in death, and smoothing it
out, he read it gently, from a student comrade. He had written briefly,
fatalistically. There could be nothing worse than all that had gone
before.

Your mother is dead these five months, one of many aged who
died from starvation. Maryna is lost. I have made careful inquiries,
but can only ascertain that she appealed to Jurka's agent in this dis-
trict at the time of the demonstration made by the royalist faction,
and was taken with other girls from Rigl and adjacent villages to the
mountain camps by the soldiers. None returned alive.

"Jurka tricked the boy," Dmitri said quietly. "He needed him in
the work here and promised in return full protection to his mother
and sister by the queen's own secret agents. This letter came to Steccho through my hands the night he took the jewels. He came to me
and told what he had seen in the Trelango apartment. Shall I speak in
detail?" He smiled most courteously at Ward.

"What you say is immaterial. I was called by Miss Trelango herself that night to complete a business transaction. I had advanced
certain sums for her musical education and training under certain
conditions to which she had agreed. She broke these conditions. It

was her own suggestion that she pay back in full her obligations to me with the jewels."

"Which were worth, let us say, about fifty times the amount you had advanced, eh?" Dmitri supplemented. "Ah, you are a financier and a very fine appraiser of values, Mr. Ward, in jewels and—otherwise. With Miss Trelango's own testimony and my own as to what my friend told me he saw and heard, there might be a difference of opinion on the price of rubies, yes?"

"Dmitri, let me end this," demanded Griffeth hoarsely. "I can't be quiet any longer."

"My boy, you are under arrest, and one call from Mr. Ward will bring his friends below. Not that I think he would call, but he might. Let me finish my story first that all may be clear to Mr. Ward, so he will not think we are deceiving him in any way. I myself told Steccho to give the jewels back to whomever he had stolen them from and to leave the service of Count Jurka. He said he could not afford to jeopardize the safety and lives of his mother and sister. This letter cleared up that point in his mind. I know he had called at the Hotel Dupont before coming to me and had left word for Jurka that he had fulfilled his mission. As you know, their two bodies were found dead in the boy Steccho's room. I myself notified Mr. Ward of this as soon as I found it out, did I not?"

Ward's face was a perfect blank. He stared at Dmitri in silence.

"I told Mr. Ward so that he would understand what had happened, and requested him to keep the entire matter silent with the police until he heard from me."

"Why did you call Mr. Ward instead of the police?" asked the Marchese sternly.

"It was not a matter for the hands of the city police. It was international in its import and should have been kept absolutely secret, but Mr. Ward thought otherwise. Doubtless he did not believe me, that I held the proofs."

"What proofs?" Carlota's hand closed over that of the old Marchese, feeling his sympathy for her.

"The proofs of Mr. Ward's private business with the queen's chamberlain. Doubtless they were not criminal; mind, I do not say they were, but I do not think that they were diplomatically ethical, shall we say, Mr. Ward?"

Ward waited, still silent and immobile, never relaxing his gaze on the face of Dmitri.

"So, and now we come to the unexpected part, when, as I tell you often, Griffeth, the gods lean down and deal the cards themselves. When I come out of my door to cross to where Steccho lived, in the gray dawn I see a closed limousine turn the corner of Third Avenue. That is most unusual for the quarter where I live, and I notice it particularly. Then I find in my friend's room the two dead bodies, both warm. Jurka was strangled by the boy and shot him in the side as they struggled. No mystery there. But the jewels for which they fought were gone, only one opal belonging to Mr. Ward in Steccho's coat pocket. I always search pockets. They are so handy for hiding things. And I find out first that whoever took those jewels did not have time or sense to look through the pockets of the dead men. Possibly he was nervous. I did look and I found several interesting things in Count Jurka's possession, his personal wallet and notebook, his keys and a letter which he had doubtless written himself to Mr. Ward before he left the hotel to find Steccho. I have that letter; it escaped the attention of the gentlemen of the police when they searched me. Carlota, my old leather music folder is there on the piano behind you, if you please, my dear." Wonderingly Carlota gave the old brown flat bag to him. He produced from it the gold-capped wallet of Jurka and several letters and documents.

"I was most fortunate in arriving at the Dupont at an hour when vigilance is relaxed. The number of the Count's suite was on his hotel key. I made my way up to that floor by the back stairs, as you say, the servants' way, and I found myself alone in his rooms. I hurried in my search of his locked trunk and desk, and I found all I wanted. And suddenly there was another key inserted in the door and Georges Yaranek came in. I stepped back behind a door and when he passed me I seized him. He is very much the stronger and I am no fighter at all, but I have to get the better of him just the same, so I use tricks. It is always permissible, is it not, Mr. Ward, when your cause is just? I take and tie him up with the heavy silk portière cords so he can do no damage, and then I find all the jewels on him, all of them. You see what a very clever precaution that is to send two out on a secret mission, and if one fails, the other he will carry it out. Georges Yaranek is no servant. He is of the Bulgarian secret service, a spy of the queen, and when Jurka came to get the jewels from Steccho, Yaranek came likewise lest the Count come not back from that house next to mine. I have his written and sworn confession of all he did, so that Mr. Ward would not feel the slightest doubt or suspicion of my word."

"Where is Yaranek?" demanded Ward. "Why was his written confession necessary? Why did you not turn him over to the police?"

"I have already told you this was an international affair, not for the city police which is very friendly to Mr. Ward, I believe. And mind, I would say this, there is something we all lose sight of in this day of upheavals. To every man his country and its cause. What is criminal to one is patriotism to another. Both Jurka and Yaranek acted most honorably according to their code. They are of the old régime, the royalists; they kill, they make war, they rob the poor, they do forever as they like, you see, and it is not wrong to them. Jurka was loyal to the old queen's interests. She ordered him to come here and find the missing jewels. For what? Not for her to wear— one wears no crowns in exile—but to convert into ready money, into gold, for immediate use. This is the hour of opportunity, mind, in Europe. Your watcher of signs sees all sorts of maneuvers not on battle-fields. The people are so hungry and harassed and deceived that they waver and do not know which side God is on. A suave and promising tongue can sway them in any direction that promises rest and safety. So with gold at her command instead of paper money, the exiled queen might seize Bulgaria. And there was only one man who would pay in cash the price of the royal rubies, so Jurka dickered with him, once he struck the right trail. That man was Ogden Ward. Oh, I have the correspondence between you, Mr. Ward," as Ward rose threateningly. "It is quite authentic, and nothing missing. Jurka had to protect himself in case of discovery, and doubtless saved the evidence in order to command your full protection. Mr. Ward agreed in writing to pay $750,000, in full for the five pieces of the collection, including the Zarathustra ruby, which is the finest pigeon-blood ruby in the world, they claim. Of course, when he found he could get them so very much cheaper, he tried himself and failed."

"But on the face of it, it is absurd," sneered Ward. "Marchese, how could these men have conveyed that amount in gold at this time to Europe without discovery?"

"Ah, that was most cleverly provided for also, by Mr. Ward," exclaimed Dmitri jocularly. "It was to have been shipped by Mr. Ward's own bankers as part of a consignment for the relief of stricken, starving Bulgaria. Count Jurka himself suggested this plan, since he was here as one of the relief committee. It was all really very touching."

"What if I say that I was aware of the whole secret plot, and merely acted as I did to betray these men, and save the rubies for Carlota Trelango?"

"It is very apt, but I am afraid it will not pass," sighed Dmitri. "The dates on these letters show your dealings with Jurka and Yaranek before you even knew that she owned the rubies."

"And where is Yaranek?" asked Ward. "Why was he not handed over to the police by you? Why was it necessary for you to have his sworn statement when he might give his own testimony? Since you were accumulating evidence against me, why not go the limit?"

"Well, I will tell you, Mr. Ward, although I do not think you will ever comprehend my motives." Dmitri sat lightly on the edge of the table and smoked slowly, happily. "I am a propagandist, but I only propagate my own propaganda, see? I have my own creed of right living and it is based upon our mutual responsibility for other people's welfare and happiness. I believe in the right to live, but I do not believe that any human group of people has any right to govern others against their will. So I fight in my own way for the small, helpless races that get crushed in the great stampede. And when I can I like to talk this way. So when I get Georges Yaranek tied and bound and I do not know what to do with him, I talk to him. First, I trust him. I loosen his hand and give him cigarettes so that we may both talk while we smoke. And I prove to him by all of Jurka's letters how he has lied to the boy Steccho and deceived him, how he has played his own game and cheated everybody else, even him, Yaranek. For look, Jurka is ambitious. The queen is old and fond of him. He wants to share the glory with no one, and so he had planned to get rid of Yaranek himself. Even while he was working with him to recover the jewels for the royalist cause, as emissary to the country from the queen to study the relief methods for starving Bulgaria, he was ready to report Yaranek to Washington for the very crime he was committing himself, collecting secret funds to promote a royal reactionary uprising. Thus he could go back alone and regret most profoundly that Yaranek, through some indiscretion, had been apprehended."

"Where is Yaranek?" asked Ward again.

"He awaits me at a certain place." Dmitri smiled at him. "We were to have sailed together. I am so very glad to announce his entire conversion to my propaganda, Mr. Ward. Of course, if you would rather we remained and conveyed our testimony to the proper government authorities, we will do so. We will not permit our plans to interfere with your wishes."

Ward strode to the window and stared out at the Square below, a conflict in his mind. He had played and lost. Not alone the jewels, but the girl he had wanted. All his life he had purchased anything that was necessary to success. He had weighed the issues of life itself in terms of gold. When he turned from the window, he asked, tersely: "What do you want?"

"I want to go back free and unhampered to my country," returned Dmitri, "with Yaranek. I want the rubies to be left unqualifiedly with Miss Trelango—"

"Dmitri, I do not want them!" Carlota cried entreatingly. "They only bring misery. You give them back for me to the people you love. They are not mine or the queen's. They belong to the children who are starving."

"The heirs of tomorrow?" smiled Dmitri whimsically. "I will gladly do so if it is your wish. Mr. Ward, you are fond of rubies. You are not interested as we are in international aspirations, shall we say, or perhaps ideals. It matters not one iota to you whether the money for these jewels goes to the royalist cause or to the feeding of those starving ones, those little victims of diplomacy, shall we call it? Will you buy these gems from Miss Trelango, and I will most gladly convey the consignment of gold to the little ones that are left alive."

"Is this your wish?" asked Ward, looking at Carlota.

Her eyes overflowed with tears. She could hardly answer as she stood between the Marchese and Griffeth.

"I should love it more than anything," she told him. "The Marchese will attend to everything for me if you are willing."

Suddenly in the doorway stood Maria, alarmed and prepared to defend her charge at any price. But Dmitri met her with one of his low, courtly bows that soothed her pride.

"Signora, you are just in time. Mr. Ward is being the bountiful fairy godfather to us all. He grants us each one what we like the best. I have a rendezvous with a friend. Mr. Ward, after you. Carlota, Griffeth, I salute love immortal!"

Jauntily he gathered up the papers and wallet into the old brown leather bag again, and handed it to the Marchese.

"Will you not personally hold these until I have sailed, and then destroy them? I make you our neutral receiver, yes? And will you not also kindly place the jewels in safe-keeping until Mr. Ward has paid for them?"

Ward passed without a word down the winding staircase ahead of him, without a backward glance at the four left in the old studio. Carlota turned to Griffeth's close embrace, weeping in deep soft sobs of relief, and the Marchese smiled at Maria.

"The leaves lie thick in the Square. They are sweeping them up to burn. Will you walk with me, Maria, and remember Vallombrosa while these children follow their own path of gold? Then we will take up the business of life once more, and put the rubies and papers in safety deposit, but for now—"

He held the door open for her, and they passed down the way that Ward had gone. Carlota lifted her head from Griffeth's shoulder.

"Heirs of tomorrow, he said," she whispered.

He kissed her lips. There seemed in their love almost a symbol of the fulfillment of years of war, of tears and bloodshed and oppression and intolerance, in what would be the dawn of a new world to those who were indeed the heirs of tomorrow.